The Caretaker's Wife

The Caretaker's Wife

Vincent Zandri

Copyright © 2019 by Vincent Zandri
Cover and jacket design by 2FacedDesign

ISBN 978-1-947993-44-0
eISBN 978-1-947993-76-1

Library of Congress Control Number: 2019937337

First hardcover edition April 2019 by Polis Books, LLC
221 River St., 9th Fl. #9070
Hoboken, NJ 07030
www.PolisBooks.com

POLIS BOOKS

"*The devil got his money's worth that night.*"
—James M. Cain, *The Postman Always Rings Twice*

"*The only thing you've got, Sheriff, is a short supply of guts.*"
—*High Plains Drifter*

Prologue

Loon Lake

February

Two years ago

They say you could hear their screams from all the way out in the road. High-pitched screams of unimaginable suffering and torture. Maybe two dozen townspeople stood outside in their mackinaws, wool watch caps, gloves, and mittens, surrounded by a bitterly cold night that was strangely illuminated in an iridescent orange/red glow by the roaring flames of a two-story house fire.

A house fire that was no accident, or so the rumors go.

The townsfolk gathered in the road and stared at the old wood house, and they were helpless to do anything about it, for fear they, too, would be burned to death. Even the sheriff, who stood tall in the center of the crowd, could do nothing. His arms hanging by his side, the brim of his cowboy hat pulled down over his eyes as if to conceal his tears, he, too, was paralyzed with grief and fear. His job was to protect the men, women, and children of Loon Lake. If he were to begin making arrests, they would all be killed. No one would be spared. His hands were tied, and his heart and soul burned along with the flesh of the four innocent souls trapped inside that doomed house.

No one dare say a single word while their cloud-like breaths rose up into the night along with the black smoke from the burning building. Not even the town's one firetruck had been summoned to the scene. What was the point? It was instead parked idly behind the sheriff's headquarters where it would remain until the house was burned to the ground.

They say you could not only hear the screams of the family—the mother, father, and their young elementary school-aged son and daughter—but you could hear some laughter too. The laughter came from two men. One voice was lower and burlier than the other. The second voice squeaked while it laughed. It was, according to the witnesses, one of the most horrible sounds one could ever hear.

The laughter was coming from the two men who started the fire and who bound the four family members to the chairs that surrounded their kitchen table. The first man, the fearless leader, was the mastermind behind the burning. The second man, his big, black leather clad right-hand goon, was the one who followed the orders to a T.

They say that while the fire began to spread in the kitchen, Fearless Leader pulled out his smartphone and began to film the family while they suffered a most horrible death. He filmed the faces of the mother and father as they writhed in pain, while the children screamed in agony. He filmed it so he could go back to it again and again and relive the torture. He even made Right-Hand Goon get in the picture along with him so that they could immortalize the event with a selfie.

So they say...

But they also say that two state trooper cruisers finally

showed up. That the yellow and blue state law enforcement officials offered a ray of hope in an otherwise bleak scenario. They say that four gray-uniformed men emerged from out of the cruisers. Three white men and one black man. All of them were said to be big men. Troopers didn't accept small men into their ranks. Only big, strong men. Only honorable men. Only brave men.

Despite the flames that were now shooting out all the windows and the roof, they say the troopers ran towards the house. They were careful to keep their backs to the people and especially the sheriff. It was as if they didn't want anyone to recognize their faces. They quickly made their way around the back and entered into the kitchen through the back door.

It's also been said that Fearless Leader wanted to take one more selfie video, this one including the troopers, before they would have no choice but to exit the burning home before the fire flashed over. If it were to flash over while they were still inside it, they would all be goners.

But no one to this day has ever seen the photos. No one has ever viewed the video documenting the deaths of the innocent family. All the people of Loon Lake Township have to go on is what they and their helpless sheriff witnessed from out on the road on that frigid February night and the rumors that soon began to spread around the little lake town that time forgot. Rumors that their town had been taken hostage by some very bad men from downstate. Gangsters, hoodlums, and blood-thirsty mobsters. The innocent men, women, and children of Loon Lake were helpless, abandoned, and perhaps even doomed, and there wasn't a thing they could do about it.

That's what they say, anyway.

1

Present Day

It was spring now, but the little house on Orchard
Grove in the North Albany suburbs had become as cold and
barren as a dead womb. The two women who'd occupied it
with me, my wife and our daughter, were not only gone but so,
too, was any sign of their physical presence. It was as if they
had died while I was away. They had died, and no one had told
me about it. Rather, no one bothered to call or write to tell me
they were in trouble or in need or want of anything. It was as
if they and their memory had been entirely erased during the
twenty long months I was away from them, living behind iron
bars, concrete, and razor wire.

But here's the reality of the matter: my wife of fifteen
years, Leslie, and our thirteen-year-old, Erin, were indeed
gone…vanished. For how long, I had no idea. But they had
taken much of their clothing with them. Also a few books
and most of their toiletries, makeup, and some odd pieces
of jewelry. When I checked inside the closet for the cash we
stored inside a strong box—five thousand dollars—it, too, was
gone. I could only assume they hadn't died or disappeared or

become abduction victims, but were, in fact, down in Palm Beach, Florida where Leslie's parents owned a condominium that overlooked the ocean.

I'd barely set my bag down on the floor of the ranch home's vestibule, and hadn't even taken my coat off yet, before the reality of their leaving began to set in. It wasn't like I expected them to greet me with open arms, having arrived home from nearly two years in Sing Sing, but it might have been nice to at least find them waiting for me. I guess I expected too much from them.

But then, where are my manners?

My name is Jonathan Kingsley. But you might know me as JA Kingsley, a variation of my Christian name I assumed at the behest of my agent back when my career was in the crapper. That was at the time when chick lit was all the rage and, at best, readers—almost all of them women, go figure—would identify me as female. At worst, the name would be dubious enough that the readers would give me the benefit of the doubt. Whatever the case, the pen name change worked, and while my name isn't up there with the Pattersons and Kings, it is not entirely anonymous either. In fact, I went on to sell quite well and even nabbed a few prestigious awards along the way.

As of late, the career stalled what with my run-in with the law. I could go into great detail about how I tossed a man through a plate glass window at Lucy's Bar after he mouthed off about my drinking. But it wasn't the drinking comment that got to me so much as the fact that he had been fucking my wife while he renovated our master bathroom. I might never have known had he not put the moves on my doctor, of all people, when he started in on a renovation of her house. When Leslie had moved out of the bedroom during the month-long renovation period, I just figured she wanted to be close to the spare bathroom. Made sense to me. But it wasn't until my doc sent me a Facebook message indicating that, in all probability, Leslie had been boning the carpenter, I was able to put two and two together.

When he showed up at Lucy's Bar one evening to collect food for him and his wife, he offered to buy me a beer. "Not that you need one," he said.

I guess that was his idea of a joke.

I smiled, thanked him, then put him down with a swift right hook that he never saw coming. I might have ended it there, but the rage took over, and my blood got hot as it sped through my veins. He was a big guy and had to be six or eight inches taller than me, but he could have been ten feet tall and it wouldn't have mattered. I just scooped him up off the floor and heaved him out the window, shattering the plate glass into a million little pieces.

Listen, I might have stopped then and there. But when I followed him outside and proceeded to bash his skull against the pavement, they all came out of the bar and pulled me off him. I guess by then I was foaming at the mouth, my eyes red and wide, my face hot and covered in sweat and little bits of his blood. He was still alive and even crying like a baby at that point, but they—the cops—still wanted to slap me with attempted murder. But here's the thing: he refused to press charges because he felt like shit for screwing my wife behind my back in the first place, especially when you took my daughter and her feelings into consideration.

I guess that was his idea of contrition.

But the Albany County DA wanted to go ahead and throw the book at me, no pun intended. In the end, we plead them down to second degree aggravated assault so long as I agreed to do three years. I got out on parole just short of two, not only because I minded my own business and kept my nose clean, but I'm told the literary workshop I ran for the more creatively inclined inmates was a model grassroots program in prison reform. The warden, a fellow Gulf War vet, shook my hand when I was finally freed and he asked me to sign a copy of my latest novel, The Bastard, for him. I signed it, "To my gracious host and fellow warrior, with affection, Kingsley."

But what all this reminded me of, oddly enough, was my writing. I'd done some in the joint, but it's not easy being creative in a place like that. It's tough concentrating on putting even two words together when you're constantly looking over both shoulders and trying to develop eyes in the back of your head. In fact, I was more anxious in prison than I had been as an Army Ranger stationed on the battlefields of Iraq during the Second Gulf War. Trust me, taking a town like Fallujah, for instance, was no picnic. I might have distinguished myself in Sing Sing with having formed a writer's workshop, but the thick, jagged scars I bore on my chest and back were proof positive that prison life was absolute hell. It was a game of survival as much as it was loneliness and despair.

Back to my first point about not being able to write in the joint. No writing for the past twenty months meant I wouldn't be getting any advances or royalties anytime soon, which meant I'd better write something pretty damn quick or I'd be starving. Truth be told, I was kind of counting on that five Gs Leslie and I had stashed away in the closet. Wasn't it just like her to steal it out from under me when I needed it most? Oh well, what the hell, I still had a credit card. It would have to do until I wrote something worthwhile. Something my agent could sell to the big New York publishers. That is, if I still had an agent.

Inside the bedroom, I started going through the drawers, looking for any kind of spare cash or change I could gather up. I would have gone through my drawers, but all my clothes had been consolidated into one bottom drawer. Pants, shirts, underwear, and socks. It also dawned on me that there were no longer any pictures of me hanging on the walls. It was as if Leslie wanted me as out of sight as much as possible.

I went through her drawers, including the one that stored her panties. I saw that she had loaded up on new stuff since I'd been gone. Silky black stuff. Nice stuff. Expensive stuff with matching bras. It made me angry because I knew now that without a doubt she was still sleeping with somebody else. Maybe even the carpenter. But somehow, just the thought of her sleeping with someone else made me hard at the same time. It had been a while since I got laid, and I never once gave in to any of those animals in the joint who will bang anything with a hole.

I looked at her picture that hung on the wall. It was a shot of her at the beach in Cape Cod. I'd taken it of her on an afternoon just after a big storm. In the picture, there's a big black cloud on the horizon. But she's smiling for the camera. Her long, dark hair is parted over her left eye, and it's blowing in the wind. She's wearing a blue, horizontally striped French sailor's shirt and loose, white trousers. I recalled how I fucked her inside the bathroom while our daughter napped in the hotel room. I remember she finished me off by taking me into her mouth and sucking the daylights out of me, swallowing me dry. Those were the days.

The picture beside that was of Erin. She'd yet to turn thirteen in the shot. She still had that cute, optimistic perkiness about her that I remember so well. It's her school picture from the fourth grade, I think. Fourth or fifth grade. There's an American flag for a backdrop behind her, and her folded hands are resting on an encyclopedia. She's looking not directly at the camera but instead, a little off to the side, like somebody called out her name at the exact moment the picture was taken. Her hair is long and black just like her mom's, and her smile is infectious. Damn, how I would miss her.

Closing up the underwear drawer, I opened the one next to it. It held Leslie's jewelry. The stuff she left behind, anyway. I grabbed a couple of sterling silver bracelets and a handful of gold rings and stuffed them in my pocket. They'd bring in maybe one hundred bucks at the pawn shop. Hell, maybe even more. Closing the drawer, I made my way to the front hall closet and went through every coat pocket. I netted three crumpled dollars and two dollars thirty-three cents in loose change.

What the hell had my world come to?

As I was closing the closet door, I saw something on the floor. It must have fallen out of a pocket while I was digging through it. It was a brochure that was partially folded, partially crumped up, as though somebody had stuffed it into their pocket and quickly forgot about it. Bending down, I picked it up and smoothed it out. It read, Loon Lake Inn, Cottages and Tavern. Below the writing was a black-and-white picture of a small pine tree covered lot with maybe a half dozen cottages on it, along with a bigger building that must have housed the tavern. I guessed the photo was taken from a boat on the water since the lot was surrounded by a pristine lake. All the cottages were made of rough pine wood by the looks of it, with asphalt shingle roofs. Each cottage had its own stone fireplace too, which made it all seem kind of cozy, peaceful, and woodsy. Below the picture was the tagline, "Peace and quiet on a trout-stocked lake. What more could you want?"

I couldn't help but smile, because I suddenly recalled where this brochure came from. I was a stickler for dragging the girls out on a Sunday, back in the days before I was sent to the joint. I'd wake everyone up early and insist they pile into the Jeep. If it was nice, I'd pull the top off, and that would just make them crankier since the wind would mess up their hair. But eventually, they would start to have fun, especially if it was a warm summer day with lots of sunshine.

It was just such a day maybe three or four years ago that we were joyriding up in the Adirondacks. We were taking the narrow winding road around Loon Lake when I happened upon a crummy old homemade sign mounted to a big old oak tree along the side of the road that said, Loon Lake Inn, one-half mile on the left. The sign also contained a black arrow pointing the way.

"Let's go check this out," I said to the girls.

"Do they have food?" Erin said.

"We'll soon see, honey," I said.

"But no drinking," Leslie said. She took hold of my free hand, squeezed it a little, to let me know she meant business.

"Maybe just one draft beer, babe," I said.

She let go of my hand and exhaled loud enough for me to hear it.

A half mile up the road, I slowed down and pulled onto a badly maintained two-track that led to the cottages. It wasn't a long road. Maybe a half mile long. But it was two-sided by old pine trees, and the damp air smelled good and fresh. Soon, the road gave way to a clearing and the entire rustic facility which had been built on it. I remember feeling a start in my heart because it looked so quaint. Like a scene Norman Rockwell might have painted. I was tempted to force the girls into staying for the night.

I stopped the Jeep and got out.

"Come on, girls," I said. "Let's go get some lunch." But they weren't budging.

"I don't like this place, Jonathan," Leslie said. "There's nobody here. It's creepy."

"I don't like it either," Erin said. She stubbornly crossed her arms over her chest, which told me she wasn't budging either. If Leslie didn't like something, Erin didn't like it. And vice versa. But the hell of it was, they were right. There were no people to be found. No vacationers on a beautiful summer's day.

No one hanging out on the small sandy beach. No one out on the lake in canoes fishing for trout. No smoke coming from the cottage chimneys. No smell of bacon and eggs frying inside the tavern. Just nothing.

"Wait here," I said.

"Hurry it up, Kingsley," Leslie said. "I want to leave this place."

I made my way across the small gravel lot to the tavern entrance. Stepping up onto a porch that ran the length of the single-story wood building, I tried to open the door. But it was locked. I pushed and pulled on it, but sure enough, it was locked. That's when I noticed the brochures. Maybe two dozen of them stuffed into a wall-mounted metal mailbox. I pulled one out, glanced at it, and then shoved it in my coat pocket.

I recall shaking my head and whispering something like, "Hell of a way to do business," as I made my way back down the porch steps. "How do they expect to make any money if they don't open their doors?"

I got back in the Jeep.

"It was locked," I said. "No one seems to be here."

"Like I said," Leslie mumbled. "Creepy. Like a Stephen King novel."

"Can we go already, Daddy?" Erin said.

I turned the Jeep around and sped back over the two-track to Loon Lake Road. While I drove, I couldn't shake the feeling that I would one day come back here, and when I did, it would be without my family.

My eyes still glued to the crumpled brochure, I couldn't help but wonder what ever happened to that little place of peace and serenity on the lake. Maybe somebody had bought it and made it operational again. It might be a good place to escape to, to write a new novel, to get my career back in order. For the first time since arriving back home, I was feeling optimistic. I made my way into the kitchen, pulled the phone off the charger, and dialed the number that appeared at the very bottom of the brochure. It rang, and I waited.

When someone picked up, it surprised the hell out of me.

"Loon Lake Inn," said a sweet voice. The voice of a young woman I immediately invented in my head. Tall, with perky breasts, beautiful brown eyes, and long hair to match. What Leslie looked like in her younger days.

She asked me how she could help.

"I'm sorry," I said, "but I didn't expect anyone to

answer."

She giggled. "And why is that?" she asked.

I told her about my visit to the property all those years ago. She giggled once more.

"That's because there wasn't anyone here," she said. "That was the summer my husband and I were buying the place. It took forever for the lawyers to seal the deal. But in the end, it all worked out just fine. Now then, would you like to make a reservation?"

Her question sort of shook me up. I guess subconsciously, I was convinced nobody would answer the phone. In my head, I pictured a wall-mounted phone ringing inside an empty tavern now filled with dust and cobwebs.

"You're married?" I said.

Jesus, what a hell of a thing to say. I'd been away for too long. My social skills had suffered.

She giggled again.

"Is that a problem?" she asked pleasantly.

I quickly gathered my wits.

"Just joking with you, mam," I said. Then, "Yes, I'd like to make a reservation for tonight if you have something."

She told me she did. When she asked me how long my stay would be, I sort of found myself looking around the kitchen and at the dining room beyond it, and the empty family room beyond that. My home screamed of loneliness and despair, and I knew in my heart that I would never be coming back here. I felt my eyes fill, and for a second or two I choked up.

Clearing the frog from my throat, I said, "Looks like I'll be staying for a while."

Vincent Zandri

2

We hung up, and I made for the front door off the vestibule. Grabbing hold of my bag, I was just about to make my way out the front door when something came over me. Turning, I made for the garage off the family room. Call it intuition, but sure enough, a big cardboard box had been placed by the door. A big box that once held rolls and rolls of paper towels. It had become moldy, probably from melted snow. During the time I'd been locked up in the joint, it had gathered lots of dust.

I opened it to find a bunch of my old books. There were some unfinished manuscripts in there too, but I didn't care about those because I knew they were garbage. What I was interested in was the typewriter that had been placed on top of everything. When I pulled it out, I could see that something was wrong with it. Some of the keys had been bent and broken, almost like somebody had purposely gone at it with a baseball bat. But then it dawned on me that someone could have just as easily dropped it by mistake while she was packing it up. The former was a definite possibility, but I wanted to believe the latter. I also searched for my laptop, but it wasn't in there.

I dropped the now useless machine back into the box, stepped into the family room and closed the door. Making my way across the dining room and kitchen, I headed down into the basement and into the laundry room. I sometimes used the place as a kind of writing studio. My laptop was set on the small desk next to the dryer. It was still plugged into the outlet. That was my good luck. I unplugged the machine, rolled up the chord and shoved the laptop under my arm, then headed back upstairs.

Back in the front vestibule, I shoved the laptop and the chord in my bag. I was ready to leave, but a strange feeling made me want to turn around one more time. A voice inside my head told me to take one final look at what had once been my entire life.

I headed for Erin's bedroom. The room was clean, the bed made, the many pillows and stuffed animals covering nearly the entire bed. Posters of boy bands were thumbtacked to the walls. The room had been painted pink, and it was very much a teenage girl's room. Her dresser was covered in makeup kits and hair brushes. Closing my eyes, I tried to remember her voice, her smell, her smile. As hard as I tried, nothing would come to me.

Stepping back out of the room, I went to the master bedroom, and stood in the open door. I locked eyes on the big bed where Leslie and I had made love hundreds of times. I saw us on the bed naked, locked in an embrace. In my head, the room was bright and filled with sunlight. But in reality, the shades were drawn, and the room was dark and foreboding like a funeral parlor.

I thought about everything that had happened in my life up to that point. Everything that had led to where I was standing right now, all alone. My whole life flashed before me in the span of an instant. I saw myself being born, saw my mother giving me up for adoption, saw the room I shared with two other boys who were not my brothers, saw myself wearing the ill-fitting hand-me-downs I wore through grammar school and most of high school. But then I saw myself growing, getting stronger. For the briefest of moments, I relived kicking some ass on the high school football field, relived mowing as many lawns as I could to get through college and then joining the Army and becoming a Ranger. I saw the platoon I lead into Falluja and I saw my men dying. In my head, I relived the hand-to-hand combat, and I recalled the black-bearded Al Qaeda fucker who cut my chest with a knife and how I used my strength to turn the knife on him. My thoughts drifted to my Army discharge and meeting Leslie, marrying Leslie, publishing my first novel—and a second and a third. Then coming up with my greatest creation of them all—Erin.

But the memories turned sour when I saw myself sleeping alone in our marriage bed while Leslie moved to the opposite side of the house…while she was cheating on me with the carpenter. I recalled the afternoon I was seated inside Lucy's Bar and I saw the carpenter walk in, and I saw myself putting him down with one solid punch. I saw myself tossing him out that window, and then I saw myself behind bars.

"So long and farewell," I said under my breath.

It was loud enough to raise the fine hairs on the back of my neck. I teared up again, and my stomach felt like someone had kicked it. About-facing, I practically ran for the front door.

I drove my Jeep to the pawn shop over on Central Avenue. There was a big neon sign outside that read, We Buy Gold and Silver. I parked in the small lot. As I was getting out, I was suddenly sorry I hadn't stuffed my pockets with more of Leslie's jewelry. I needed it more than she did at this point, and what the hell, most of it I'd purchased on her behalf. I made my way into the shop. It was filled with all sorts of junk stacked on shelves. Everything from electric guitars to full sets of used luggage. Some of the more valuable stuff like jewelry and handguns were kept inside a long glass counter.

A man appeared from out of the back. He was a big man, his round face sporting a goatee and mustache. He was chewing something like I'd caught him in the middle of a very early lunch.

"Help you?" he asked.

I reached into my coat pockets, pulled out the jewelry I'd snatched from Leslie's drawer, and set it all atop the counter. He swallowed whatever was in his mouth. Then he looked at the jewelry. He fingered the pieces with his sausage-thick fingers. When he was through, he looked into my eyes.

"What do you want for this stuff?" he said.

I cocked my head over my shoulder.

"I was hoping three-hundred," I said.

But I had no idea what used jewelry was worth. All I knew was I needed the cash. Needed it bad.

He picked at the food stuck in his front teeth with the long nail on his index finger. Then he snickered and grinned. It told me I was asking either way too much or way too little. Behind him, mounted to the wall, was a round mirror wrapped in a kind of ornate gold frame. I saw my face inside it. Round, shaven, my brown eyes looking sad. My hair had gone somewhat gray in prison. But at least I still had it. I also had strength. Prison was the perfect poison if you enjoyed nothing but time, and I used a lot of that time to hit the weight yard. I'd grown solid in prison. More than solid. My muscles had burst out of my skin, and I was proud of them now. In a word, I looked badass.

"So, what'll it be?" I said. "We have a deal?"

That's when I saw it displayed only a couple of feet away from the mirror. A typewriter set on a metal shelf. Three typewriters, in fact. But it was the one closest to the mirror that captured my full attention. I still preferred to write on a good old-fashioned portable manual typewriter than I did my laptop computer. There was something about the sound of the keys smacking the paper. The rat-tat-tat, machine gun-like rhythm. I wasn't a typewriter expert by any means. But by the looks of things, the machine was a late 1960s era Olivetti.

"How much for the Olivetti?" I asked.

"What's an Olivetti?" he said.

From experience, I knew that a vintage Olivetti could run you five-hundred bucks. It was a stroke of luck that he didn't know one typewriter from another.

"The one on the far right," I said. "Does it work?"

He nodded. "Perfect working order. They all are."

"I'll give you fifty bucks for it," I said.

He pursed his lips, went to the cash register, and opened it. He pulled out two Benjamins and a US Grant, which he set down on the glass case before me. He then went to the shelf, pulled down the Olivetti typewriter, and set that down next to the cash.

"Three-hundred for the jewelry," he said. "Minus the typewriter."

I took the cash and shoved it in my pocket.

"You got a spare sheet of blank paper?" I asked.

He told me to hang on while he made his way over to the copy machine. He opened the paper drawer and stole a sheet. He came back and handed it to me.

"This thing is a relic, you ask me," he said.

I shoved the paper into the spool, then placed my fingers on the keys. I typed, This thing is a relic, you ask me.

"You're pretty quick with that thing," he said. "You a writer?"

"Used to be." I smiled. "Hope to be again."

"How long you been outta the joint?" he asked. The question took me by surprise.

"How'd you know?"

"I can always tell. You didn't get that build at the local Planet Fitness. Did seven years myself at Green Haven for two counts of larceny. But that was in another life."

"Just got out," I said.

"Thus the need for quick cash," he said. "You got that look on your face that tells me you plan on going somewhere. Your parole officer know about that shit?"

"I'm not going far," I said. "Just up into the mountains."

"You ain't gotta report to a halfway house?"

"Lawyer worked out a sweet deal for me. Just can't leave the country for a while. They want me to work, but who the hell hires ex-cons? That's why I need the typewriter."

"Maybe you'll write something that'll make you famous. A prison memoir. That's it, a prison memoir."

I pulled the typewriter off the counter, cradled it under my arm. It felt heavy and solid and wonderful. It was my portal to a new future.

"Not a bad idea," I said. "I'll be seeing you."

"Keep your nose clean, pal," he said.

"It was never dirty in the first place," I said, opening the door and walking out.

Setting the Olivetti onto the shotgun seat, I took off my leather coat and placed it over the typewriter. Now down to a snug-fitting black t-shirt, I drove to the grocery store and bought two reams of blank copy paper, some lunch meat, white bread, a half dozen cans of Campbell's chicken noodle soup, a jar of peanut butter, a dozen eggs, a carton of orange juice, a carton of milk, and finally a twelve pack of beer—cans, of course. I paid with cash, left the store, and stored everything into the back of the Jeep. That's when, out the corner of my eye, I spotted Lucy's Bar at the bottom of the hill. The window I'd tossed the carpenter out of was now repaired. Had been for some time, or so I assumed. I don't know why exactly, but I felt a smile growing on my face, because once upon a time, someone very special worked at the bar. I couldn't help but wonder if she was still employed there.

Getting back behind the wheel of the Jeep, I turned the engine over and backed out of the lot. I knew I should be hitting the highway since it was already past noon, but I couldn't help myself. I wanted to make a quick pit stop to my old haunt. Rather, I felt the need to make a pit stop.

I parked right in the front of the joint. It was spring. The air was still cool, but some folks were seated at the tables on the deck. As I walked in, some of them looked at me, but I didn't recognize their faces, and I wasn't sure they recognized mine. But it was a different story when I walked into the bar. It was dark despite the sunshine outside.

A few of the regulars were bellied up to the horseshoe-shaped bar. Richie, the old Marine gunny sergeant, was one of them. He was dressed in a loose-fitting, flower-pattern Tommy Bahama button-down shirt. He might have been in his mid-seventies by now, but the solid as granite muscles in both his arms would have made Popeye jealous. Seated dutifully on the stool beside him was his longtime girlfriend, Sandie. She had short strawberry blonde hair and a perfect rack that was accentuated by a low-cut sweater.

"Well, look at what the cat just dragged in," she said as soon as she laid eyes on me.

That got the bartender's attention. His name was Stan, and he was a short but muscular Pollock who wore his white hair brush cut short. I knew that he played college ball, and he was every bit as tough as the pigskin he used to cradle into end zone after end zone. Stan had supported my side in the... let's call it altercation...with the carpenter, so his eyes lit up at my presence.

"Kingsley," he said. "Word on the street was that you were dead."

I sat down at the bar, nodded at Richie and Sandie. The muscular gunny sergeant nodded back and immediately refocused on the Lotto Quickdraw playing out on the wall-mounted flat screen.

"Maybe I am dead," I said, "and this is heaven."

"Oh hell," Stan said. "Because if this is heaven, I wanna get the hell out."

I ordered a beer. A draft.

"Listen," he said, leaning in closer to me, "I'll serve you. But if Lucy comes in, you're gonna have to leave." Lucy being the owner of the joint.

I pictured the moment I tossed the carpenter through the window. The sounds of shattering glass and a heavy body falling to the pavement outside once more rang in my ears.

The window alone probably cost Lucy fifteen hundred bucks.

Maybe it was insured.

"I get it, Stan," I said.

He poured me my beer, set it in front of me.

"You here to see Theresa?" he asked a bit sheepishly.

"She still working the job?"

"Somebody's got to put food on the table for her husband and kid," Stan said.

I felt like something poked me in the gut.

"She got married?"

"To the asshole," Stan said. "Brian. If you can believe it." I guess I could believe it. Why did grown men and women insist on falling in love with the people they should stay away from?

"Where is she?" I asked.

"Down in the basement counting out her tips." He glanced at his watch. "Lucy ain't due back for a half hour you wanna take a walk down to see her. I heard you got divorced while you were in the can. Means you're free as a bird."

"News to me," I said, seeing my empty house in my head.

Were divorce papers on their way soon?

Stan gave me a wink. I drank some beer, slid off the stool, and headed for the basement stairs.

The basement was cramped and dimly lit. There were all sorts of kegs hanging around, plus some palates filled with cases of beer and wine. A small office was located in the back. The door was open so I could see her seated at the desk. Her back was to me, and the way her long dark hair draped her shoulders broke my heart. I knew she had it rough, and I knew the tips she was counting on to survive was like stacking pennies. You'd never get rich working for Lucy. But at least it was a job. Something her new husband, Brian, had trouble hanging on to.

That was his reputation anyway.

My footsteps were silent. Entering the office, I wrapped my hands gently around her eyes.

"Guess who?" I said.

It was impossible for me to see the smile on her pretty face, but I could feel it all right. She turned, stood, and wrapped her arms around me. She hugged me like nobody's business. I kissed her neck and smelled the sweet lilac scent on her skin and her smooth, clean hair, and I swear, I felt her beating heart.

"Just now," I said. "Today."

She released me and took a step back.

"Let me get a look at you, Kingsley," she said. "You've lost some weight. And my God, where'd you get all those muscles?"

"Lots of time on my hands," I said. "I put it to good use."

She was wearing her tight black Lucy's Bar outfit, and her eyes were big and wet, and one of them was black and purple. She'd done her best to make-up the hell out of it, but I could still make it out. I gently touched it with my thumb.

"What happened?" I said. "It was him, wasn't it?"

She wouldn't admit it, but then, she didn't deny it either. "He's my husband," she said. "I probably deserved it."

"Nobody deserves that," I said, feeling the rage enter into my bloodstream. I had to watch it, or else I'd begin shaking, and that would scare her.

"Let's not talk about that," she said. "How are you now that you're free again?"

"I'm okay," I said. "I'm leaving."

Her smile got lost.

"Where? You only just got home. What about your wife? Your daughter?"

"They left me. Or haven't you heard?"

Her smile returned, ever so slowly. She wrapped her arms around my neck and laid the sweetest kiss ever on me. It was all I could do to come up for air.

"I want you," she said. "Take me right here. Right now. I don't care."

"We can't," I said. "And you know it, Theresa."

"Why is it always, 'We can't'? Why doesn't that ever change? Your wife cheated on you, and now she's left you."

"I wouldn't cheat then, and neither will you now, no matter how we feel about one another."

"But your wife is gone."

"But you're married now, remember?" I touched her eye again. "Even if he is an asshole."

She was quiet for a bit.

"How's your boy?" I asked.

"He's okay."

I pictured the scruffy-haired, chubby little guy in my head. He must have been four or five by now. She had him with her now husband back when they were just dating. Like his mom, the little guy had it rough, whether he was aware of it or not. I dug into my pocket, pulled out the cash, and peeled off a fifty.

"This is for your son," I said. "Don't let Brian take it away from you."

She wiped a tear from her cheek, nodded, and took the cash. I knew it was way more than she would be taking home in tips. I also knew her husband wasn't working. Or if he was, he was fast on his way to not working anymore. His was a life of cheap beer and time-sucking video games and abuse. Oh, but ain't love grand.

I kissed her again like I meant it.

The Caretaker's Wife

"I'll be checking in on you from time to time, Theresa," I said. "I promise not to disappear entirely."

She turned. "Wait," she said.

I stopped. "What is it?"

"What if I divorce him?"

"Leave Brian?" I said. "Is that what you really want?"

"Yes," she said. She wiped another tear from her good eye.

"I'll be seeing you, kid," I said, and then made my way back up the stairs.

When I went back into the bar to finish my beer, Lucy was standing at the entry.

"Oh no you don't, Kingsley," she said. She opened the door. "Out you go."

Lucy was a small woman with salt and pepper hair. But she was still a force to be reckoned with. I nodded at Stan and the others at the bar. They nodded back. I wondered if I'd ever see them again. I wondered if it mattered all that much. There was nothing left for me here.

I walked out.

"Don't let the door slap me in the ass, Lucy," I said.

"And don't come back, you here?" she said.

3

Driving. Highway 87. Northbound.

The road was empty this time of day, and the cool air felt good slapping at my face while the Jeep radio blared some classic rock. The Eagles. Reminded me of high school. Drinking and smoking pot in some kid's basement. Hiding the bong as soon as the folks came through the door after work, them pretending not to notice our red eyes or the pot smoke when they came down to check on us. Those were the days, my friend.

I thought about Leslie and Erin, and I also thought about Theresa, and I wondered if I would ever get it right with women. I wasn't getting any younger, but the women were becoming more and more of a mystery to me. They were made of solid granite, and I'd become a dull chisel. I might have carved out some serious muscles on the Sing Sing weight platform, but when it came to women, I didn't stand a chance at carving out a life of love, fulfillment, and happiness. That's how I felt anyway.

"...what a woman can do to your soul," sang the Eagles. Having just spent almost two full years behind bars, I had no idea what it felt like to be with a woman anymore. Leslie had moved out of the bedroom long before I got sent up to Sing Sing. During my trial, she would hardly look at me. If she did look at me, it was with a scowl on her face. It reeked of hatred. It was a tough thing to swallow. She had been the one to cheat on me. She alone made the decision to sleep with the carpenter and yet, while I was going through the trial and watching what had been a substantial bank account rapidly fall into the red, I felt like I was the one who had wronged her. Leslie was a master at turning the tables on you. When she was mad at me, then Erin would be mad at me. It was a house of horrors because life became me versus the women I loved with all my heart.

By the time I was convicted in a court of law, handcuffed, and escorted out of the courtroom by two burly Albany County sheriff's deputies, I almost felt relieved. At least I wouldn't have to suffer Leslie's sneers anymore. But then, as I made my way past her and Erin on my way out the courtroom door, I didn't notice any tears streaming down their cheeks. I didn't see any sadness on their faces. I didn't see scowls or frowns. Instead, I saw something else. I saw smiles. My wife and daughter smiled at me as I was dragged past them on my way to a maximum security prison.

I drove into the sunshine, and unless I had to, I avoided the rearview mirror entirely. With each passing mile, I felt the weight of Sing Sing—its iron bars, concrete, and razor wire—disappear. In my head, I might have been picturing the faces of my wife and daughter, but the more miles I placed between them and me, the better I felt. An hour and a half later, I exited the highway for Loon Lake Road. It was exactly the way I remembered it from a few years ago when I had the girls with me in the Jeep. The road was winding and narrow, and I took in the good smell of the tall pines that lined both sides of it. As I drove the narrow, winding road that followed the perimeter of the lake, I breathed in the fresh air, and I felt happier and freer than I'd felt in years. Soon, I came upon a sign that advertised Loon Lake Inn. It was the same sign I'd come upon years ago, only it had been given a fresh coat of paint and a new look.

Below Loon Lake Inn was a black on white sketching of the tavern and the cottages, complete with smoke billowing from the chimneys. Below that it read, Peaceful cottages and fine dining. Like the old sign, there was a black arrow that pointed the way. Written above the arrow were the words, one-half mile.

I couldn't help but smile. I recalled the pleasant voice of the woman who spoke to me on the phone just a few hours before. Maybe she was as attractive as she sounded. I already knew she was friendly. Never before had I slept in one of Loon Lake Inn's beds, but for some reason, I felt like I was going home. I felt as if all the roads I'd traveled in my life up to this very point in time led here.

The long, two-track had been updated with a well-maintained gravel drive. But the trees that bookended the road were just as thick and damp as they were the first time I drove through here. This time when I came upon the clearing, I didn't get the sense that the inn had been abandoned. Instead, I got the feeling of it being very much alive.

I parked the Jeep beside an old blue Ford F-150 pickup and got out. Smoke was rising up from the tavern's stone chimney. From where I was standing, I could smell something good coming from the kitchen. It smelled like home cooking. After twenty months of prison food, you have no idea how good the smell was. I took a quick look around. Some canoes were parked on the beach for whoever wanted to use them. The lawn had been freshly cut and the cabins, although rustic, looked well maintained with new green asphalt rooves on each of the eight units. The swing set and the kid's jungle gym had been given a fresh coat of paint. The place was old and probably dated back to the 1920s or '30s, but to me, it looked brand new. It made me wonder why there weren't more guests. Or any guests for that matter. But then, it was still very early in the season. Even the lake would be too cold for swimming. The guests would be coming as soon as the weather turned hot.

I made my way over a small stone path to the tavern, climbed the steps up onto the porch. The wood door was open and made to stay that way with a big rock placed at its bottom. A screen door separated the interior from the exterior. The hinges squeaked when I pulled it open and stepped inside.

To my left was a dark wood counter, and mounted to the wall behind it were a bunch of small wooden boxes that held the keys to the cabins. By the looks of it, there was an office located beyond the desk.

To my right was the tavern. It had a long old wood bar, and multiple shelves of bottled liquor took up most of the space on the bar back wall, and there was a dining area that supported four round tables. Behind those, four more booths were pressed against the wall. Past the bar was the kitchen. Even though it smelled like something good was cooking, the place was empty.

I went to the wood counter, rang the bell. It was strange because even though I didn't notice any closed circuit TV cameras mounted to the ceiling or ceiling corners, I couldn't shake the feeling of being watched. It was something you developed in the joint. The feeling of constantly being watched. If nothing else, prison was a fishbowl, and you were the little goldfish trying to steer clear of the hungry sharks.

When she emerged from the back office, I felt my stomach cramp up. She was of average height, maybe in her late thirties or early forties, with thick dark if not black hair that was parted over her left eye and ended at her shoulders.

Her face was long, but not too long, and her eyes were like big brown pools. Her nose couldn't have been more perfectly sculpted if Michelangelo had carved it out of the best Italian marble. She was wearing a loose-fitting denim button-down that was unbuttoned just enough to reveal a hint of her black bra, and she wore two sterling silver necklaces, one of which contained a cherub pendant. Her Levis jeans were tight and fit her hips like a second skin. Her cowboy boots were brown and worn and the perfect accent to the rest of her outfit. And yes, I was able to capture all this in the time it took her to walk the ten or so feet from her office to the front counter.

Here's the thing: not only was she a knockout in every sense of the word, she reminded me of Leslie. Not the same way in which Theresa bore a vague resemblance to her. But more like the resemblance was uncanny. Maybe the woman standing before me wouldn't have qualified as Leslie's twin sister, but for certain, she could have passed as her younger sister. She must have noticed me staring at her because she shot me a curious look.

"Can I help you, sir?" she said. Her voice was as pleasant as it had been over the phone just a little while ago.

I guess it took me a while to form my words because she scrunched her brow and pursed her lips.

"Sir," she repeated. "Can I help you?"

I shook my head, and quickly got my shit together.

"Yes," I said, clearing my throat and taking a step forward. "I spoke with you earlier on the phone."

"Excuse me," she said like a question, pulling up on her shirt sleeves so that her sterling silver bracelets clanged together.

"On the phone," I said. "I called about a reservation." She giggled then.

"Now we're getting somewhere," she said. "What did you say your name was?"

I told her my name, then pulled out my wallet and showed her my credit card just to prove it. She then told me her full name, and when she shook my hand, I wanted to hold onto hers forever.

"Oh yes," she said, taking back her hand. "I remember speaking with you, Mr. Kingsley. You're early in the season. Most of our customers don't arrive until next month when it gets hot and all the schools get out. But if you like seclusion, you'll love Loon Lake Inn."

"Yes, Cora," I said. "I plan on getting some writing done."

Her face lit up then. I was hoping it would light up. Some women are suckers for writers. They romanticize them. I wanted her to be one of those women.

"So you're a writer?" she said, her voice and face filled with wonder. "How cool. I've always wanted to write a book, but I can't even spell my own name." She giggled sweetly. "What kind of writing do you do?"

"Mysteries mostly," I said. "Hard-boiled ones."

"Anything I've read?"

That was always the distressing part about telling people what I did for a living because most people hadn't heard of me. But I was hoping to change all that with the book I would write up here. I told her the name of a couple of paperback books I had written, and she slowly shook her head at each title. But then she told me she would look up my name online and order something. If she liked it, she'd order a few copies for the tavern.

"People tend to gather in here to drink coffee and chill by the big fireplace on rainy days," she explained. "Be good to have some thrilling reading material to keep them occupied."

"Great," I said, truly loving the idea.

"So, how long are planning on staying, Mr. Kingsley, if you're planning on writing a book here?"

"I don't really have a departure date in mind," I said. "I don't have a place to live at the moment, so I was sort of hoping we could maybe make a deal for an extended stay."

For a long beat, she looked not at me, but through me. Like she was trying to figure out how my insides worked. Like the clockmaker who's peeled back the metal backing on a pocket watch, she was trying to see what made me tick.

"Well, it just so happens we have one cabin that contains a galley kitchen that's located just a little off campus, if you will."

"Off campus?"

"Meaning it's not clustered with the other eight. It's a short walk via a narrow path through the pine woods to the north. We usually advertise it for honeymooners for obvious reasons, but so far you're the first bite."

"God knows I'm no longer a honeymooner," I said, not without a laugh.

"Yes, time does fly by," she said. "Are you married, Mr. Kingsley?"

"Not anymore," I said. "Rather, I'm going through a divorce. Or about to be anyway."

For another long moment, she just looked at me. Looked into my eyes. I couldn't tell if the expression on her face was one of happiness or confusion. All I knew was that it was beautiful.

"Like they say," she said after a beat, "it's complicated."

"Exactly," I said. Then, "And you, Cora? You mentioned on the phone that you were married."

"That she is," barked the gruff voice behind me.

I turned quickly. The man standing there four-square in a long food-stained apron had a scowl on his face. Or what I interpreted as a scowl anyway. He had to be in his late fifties or early sixties. He wasn't tall, but he was thick in the shoulders, barrel-chested, and his round gut was no stranger to beer. His face hadn't seen a razor in a few days, and his salt and pepper hair was receding rapidly.

"I'm Sonny, Cora's husband, and Loon Lake Inn owner and caretaker." He wiped his meaty hand off on his apron. "Sonny Torchi is the name, and I aims to please thee." He smiled when he said that last bit, like it was his standard corny rhyme.

"Nice to meet you, Sonny," I lied, taking his hand in mine.

Unlike his wife's hand, I couldn't wait to release his. He was one of those guys who's older than you, but tries to assert his dominance by squeezing your hand so hard you feel like your bones are about to get crushed. It was a hand that knew the importance of hard, physical labor. Also a hand that wanted to hurt mine. But my hand was just as strong, and I let him know it by squeezing even harder.

When I finally pulled my hand free from his, he grinned.

"You're a strong one," he said.

"I try to keep in shape," I said, recalling the countless bench presses I performed in the rec yard.

"Did you have lunch?" he asked, his tone suddenly pleasant and welcoming. "Plenty leftover."

The smell coming from the kitchen was damn good. I hadn't eaten much of anything since my release from the joint early this morning. I wasn't exactly looking forward to digging in to one last prison breakfast. Lunch sounded like a fine idea.

And what the hell, maybe Cora would join me.

"Sure," I said. "That would be terrific."

"I'll be seeing you in the tavern, Mr. Kingsley," Sonny said.

He turned and left. That left me alone again with Cora. I wasn't much for fantasizing about women. It was one of those things you avoided in the joint. Because the more you thought about them, about their nakedness and their perfect titties and trimmed pussies, the lonelier you got. Also, the hornier and more frustrated. Being horny inside the joint was a dangerous thing. Sure, you could always find a quiet corner to relieve yourself, but some poor souls resorted to putting it in a man. I resisted that kind of temptation, and I was proud to say that, although I was nearly beaten to death once, no one ever violated me. In that sense, I was as pure and innocent as a newborn baby.

But standing there at the counter, I couldn't help but undress Cora with my eyes. I knew she was wearing a black pushup bra. I wondered if her panties were black. Maybe she was wearing a thong. Maybe her pussy was wet. I breathed in, and I tried to smell her. If I could have, I would have come around the counter, pulled down her jeans, and put it to her right there on the spot. Like I said, it'd been a long, long time since I enjoyed the affection of a beautiful woman, and I could bet it showed on my face.

She proceeded to run my card while I heard the sound of Sonny setting up a place for me at the bar. She grinned at me while she ran the card through the machine, not once but twice, and then a third time. After the third try, she shook her head and frowned.

"I'm sorry, Mr. Kingsley," she said. "But I'm afraid your card is being declined. Do you have another one I can try?"

I felt a start in my heart and a wave of ice cold washed up and down my back. It never dawned on me that my credit card might not work any longer. Leslie had access to the card. Had she maxed it out while I was in prison? A definite possibility if not a probability.

"There must be some mistake, Cora," I said, just to make myself look like the victim.

She tried it one more time. Same result.

"No," she said. "Definitely declined." Handing me back the card. "Do you happen to have any cash?"

I grinned, but not happily. Digging into my jeans pocket, I pulled out what was left of my cash. About one hundred sixty bucks.

"That's all I've got to my name, I'm sorry to say."

"I don't want to take your last bit of cash," Cora said.

"I'm hoping to make more very soon," I said. "I had no idea about my credit card, or I wouldn't have made the reservation in the first place." I shook my head in embarrassment. "I feel like such a dope."

"Maybe you can call your bank and see if they'll extend you more credit," Cora offered.

But it was all useless. The realization had sunk in pretty fast. There was no mistake, and no banker in their right mind was going to offer me, an ex-con with no job, any credit. Why? Because not only had my wife maxed the card out, I could bet she hadn't paid the monthly bill in forever either. Now she was gone.

"Soup's on," Sonny called from the tavern.

I was grateful for the distraction.

"Tell you what, Mr. Kingsley," Cora said. "Why don't you grab some lunch and we'll figure something out later."

"You're sure, Cora?" I said.

"I'm quite sure," she said, coming around the counter.

"Will you be joining me for lunch?" I asked hopefully.

"I already ate," she said. "But I can sit with you if you like." She glanced at her watch. "It's pretty quiet around here this time of year, and it's about beer o'clock after all."

"You start early up here," I said.

"Are you kidding," she said, touching my forearm gently with her fingertips. "It's getting late."

4

I sat on a stool inside the tavern. Cora sat on the stool to my right, and Sonny stood across from me behind the bar. He was still wearing his stained apron. He'd served me a bowl of homemade venison stew that came from a buck he claimed to have shot near the lake last fall. He pointed to the deer head mounted above the fireplace. It was an eight pointer. I wasn't much of a deer hunter, but it looked like a fine trophy to me.

I dug into the stew. It was piping hot and delicious. It had been served with some homemade cornbread and a tall draft beer in a frosty mug. I'd forgotten that food could taste so good, and I attacked it with vigor.

Sonny poured himself a beer. He drained half the mug with his first swig.

"When was the last time you ate, Mr. Kingsley?" he asked, wiping the foam from his lips with the back of his hand. Setting down the mug, he pulled a vape pen out from under his apron and took a long drag off of it. "Must be that a healthy appetite like yours got you those muscles."

I came up for air, wiped my mouth with the cloth napkin.

"I missed breakfast," I said. "Guess I didn't realize how famished I really am."

I drank some beer. It was good and ice cold.

"You come from down around Albany?" Sonny went on.

"He's a writer," Cora said before sipping on her own cold draft. "A novelist."

Sonny put his vape device away and exhaled a cloud of blue steam.

"You don't say," he said. "What kind of books?"

"Mysteries mostly," I said.

"I thought we might put some copies of Mr. Kingsley's books in the tavern, Sonny. You know, like in case of rainy days."

Sonny gave her a look. I wasn't sure what to read in the look, but to me, it didn't seem like he was overly pleased with the idea. Judging by the way his face went tight, I'd say he looked downright jealous. I decided to bury my face in the wonderful stew.

"Tell me something, Mr. Kingsley," he said after a time, "how long were you planning on staying?"

"Indefinitely," Cora broke in. "He's writing a new book while he's here."

She drank some more beer, wiped her pretty mouth with the back of her hand.

"He is, is he?" Sonny said. "Could be some good publicity for the inn. A big shot writer penning his new book at Loon Lake Inn where peace and serenity is our motto."

"And good venison stew, too," I added.

I guess that's when Cora decided there was no better time to mention my not so little credit card dilemma.

"Mr. Kingsley's credit card seems to be out of date, Sonny," she said. "Maybe we can work something out with him. You know, in exchange for rent."

Sonny furrowed his brow, and his face turned red. It was like he was reading some kind of underlying meaning in his wife's idea. Or maybe even like he'd faced this same situation before. He was a lot older than his wife, who was an absolute knockout. He wasn't exactly Johnny Depp anymore. And he was way out of shape. He had to have known that Cora could do a lot better if she wanted to. He pulled out his vape device again and took a big hit from it. I guess whatever he was smoking helped to calm him down.

"Normally, I'd say no credit card, no cabin," he said after a long beat. "But if what Cora says is true…that you're a famous writer or something…it might help with publicity for folks to know you chose Loon Lake Inn to write your next book. We could take pictures of you working and put it up on the website."

"Wonderful," Cora chimed in, a cheery smile on her face.

If I didn't know any better, she seemed awfully eager for me to become a permanent part of Loon Lake Inn. Their main attraction even.

"Not so fast, honey," Sonny added. "Mr. Kingsley might have some clout as a writer, but food and lodging don't come cheap, and to be honest, I could use another strong back around here to help with the caretaking." He vaped away and stared at me. "That is you don't mind a little man's work, Mr. Kingsley. You being used to sitting around on your brains all day. Be a shame to waste all those muscles."

If only he knew the work I did in the prison laundry every morning, day in and day out, he wouldn't have posed such a smug-ass question. Washing shit, cum-stained bedsheets and pillowcases, the searing temperatures inside the facility, the constant fear of some radical Muslim or Aryan sneaking up on you from behind and shoving a shank in your gut. You had to always be putting those eyes in the back of your head to good use. You had to be aware of everything going on all around you while you busted your ass, shoving linens in and out of those damn machines. I might have told Sonny all about my experience working with my hands in the joint, but my gut was telling me it was better that he not know anything about my past. Not if he planned on letting me live here on Loon Lake for a while.

"You're right, Sonny," I said. "But when I was a young man, I worked construction sites. I also mowed a lot of lawns and shoveled a lot of driveways. I'm no stranger to getting my hands dirty and my brow sweaty. I'd be happy to help out."

"My wife and I are in the process of buying most of the property along the north side of the lake," he said, like I should be impressed. "The rest of the property is owned by the state. They allow us access to the trails if we maintain them. Our guests love hiking the trails. It's the top special activity next to fishing and swimming."

I finished up the last of the stew and sopped up the rest of the juices with the final piece of cornbread. I popped it in my mouth and washed it all down with my last ounce of beer. I was so hungry, I swear I could have gone for another round of everything. But since I wasn't paying for anything, I thought I'd best not push the envelope.

"What my husband is trying to ask you, Mr. Kingsley," Cora said, setting her hand on my thigh, "is would you mind helping him with clearing the trails? It's tough work. But it can also be fun."

I nodded. "Sure," I said. "I'd be happy to. So long as it means I can enjoy more of your terrific home cooking, Sonny."

"What about you, Mr. Kingsley?" he said. "You know how to cook? We could also use some help in the tavern."

"Sonny," Cora chimed in, "Mr. Kingsley is here to write a book. We can't take up all his time treating him like an indentured servant." When she squeezed my thigh, I thought I might jump off my stool. "Now, can we?"

She shifted her eyes to mine. Her eyes were somewhat glazed over now that she had a full beer in her. It got me to thinking that Cora was one of those women who changed when she started drinking. She entered into a kind of altered state that, in some cases, brought out the best in people. But more often, it could bring out the worst. In Cora's case, I was guessing that it brought out her wilder side. Judging by the look on Sonny's already red face, I could tell he didn't like her stepping on his toes. He also didn't like where she had set her hand. She quickly got the message and removed it.

"Not a problem," I interjected. "I'm no cook, but I know my way around a bar. I can tend at night if that helps. I don't write at night anyway."

Sonny smiled. "Great!" he bellowed, issuing a squeaky laugh. He reached over the bar and slapped my arm so hard I thought I might fall to the floor. "You can start tomorrow night. We sometimes get a couple of regulars from Crown Point who come in after fishing."

Cora slipped off her stool. "Come on, Mr. Kingsley," she said. "I'll show you to your cabin."

"Thanks for lunch, Sonny," I said.

"Don't thank me," he said. "You're gonna work for it. Trust me."

I didn't like the way he grinned when he said it. But then, what the hell could I do? I was broke, and broke men didn't have a leg to stand on. Then again, what he didn't know was that my volunteering to bartend meant I could sample the liquor at my leisure. Broke men didn't have money for booze either.

"By the way, everyone," I said, "if we're going to be living and working together, I want you to call me just plain Kingsley. All my friends do."

What I didn't tell them was that I didn't really have many friends anymore. Stan at Lucy's, and Theresa, of course. But that was about it.

"Okay, Kingsley it is," Sonny said. "See you 'round five

tomorrow night to open the bar for happy hour. I'll let you sleep in tomorrow morning seeing as you just got here, but the morning after that, I'll get you at five-thirty in the AM. We hit the trails at dawn."

Just the mere thought of getting out of bed in the dark filled me with a dread so profound I thought my lunch would come back up on me. But then, I needed to look on the bright side. Just this morning I woke up in the dark on a stiff cot inside Sing Sing. Now, I had a new home on a pristine lake, and by God, if a perfect piece of ass didn't accompany it. Only thing now was to see how far I could go with that perfect piece of ass without getting myself killed in the process.

I slid off my stool.

"Ready, Cora?" I said.

"Let's grab your things," she said.

Her voice was chipper and happy, like my sudden presence at Loon Lake Inn was the best thing to happen to her in ages.

5

I grabbed my bag, my leather coat, and the box of groceries out of the Jeep. Cora volunteered to carry my typewriter.

"A real typewriter," she said. "You don't see these much anymore."

"Most writers like to write on laptops," I said as we approached a narrow trail that led from the eight main cottages, across the lawn towards the pine woods. "I like to use a typewriter because you feel the words coming out of your fingers while you type them. You feel like you're a part of the story, instead of just the jerk telling it."

"That's a beautiful thought," she said as we entered under the shady canopy of the forest. "You become a character in your own book. What an intriguing thought, Kingsley."

We walked the trail for maybe three minutes until we came to another small clearing. Set in the center of the clearing was a cabin that was a little bigger than the other guest cabins. It also had its own access to the lake, including its own little beach. Cora balanced the typewriter on one arm while pulling a key from her pocket. She stepped up onto the small front porch, shoved the key in the lock, and opened the door. Making her way inside, I followed.

It was a compact but pleasant cabin with a fireplace to the right, and to the left, bunk beds were built into the wall. A small table and a couple of chairs occupied the center of the floor. A couch was set before the fireplace.

Toward the back of the cabin, I could make out a kitchenette and even a small bathroom. It was a cozy space not that much larger than a hotel room, but knowing that I no longer had a home or the women who filled it, it looked like a mansion to me…my refuge from the disaster that had become my life.

Cora set the typewriter on the table. Stepping over to the bunk beds, I set my bag, coat, and groceries down on the bottom bunk. Unzipping the bag, I grabbed the ream of blank paper and set that on the table beside the typewriter.

For a beat or two, we both stared at the novel that had yet to be written.

"Now, all I have to do is come up with the words," I said.

"I'm sure you'll think of something," she said. "Geniuses like you always do."

I hardly knew the woman, and she was calling me a genius. If she was trying to flatter me, it was working. I'd needed an ego boost right around then. When she made her way into the kitchen, I couldn't help but lock eyes on her ass—the way it was so perfectly packed into her worn Levis. I felt myself getting excited. I was falling hard for Cora. You could almost feel the tension inside the cabin. I knew she had to have been feeling it too.

Opening the small refrigerator, she pulled out two bottles of beer and uncapped them with an opener she pulled out of a wood drawer.

"Beer in the fridge," I said. "I've definitely hit pay

dirt."

She smiled. "I keep a cold six-pack in here at all times," she said. "I like to come out here when I want to get away from it all and just be by myself." She paused and stared at the wall like she was looking off into the distance. "Sonny, he can be…"

"You don't have to explain," I said. "I get it." Then, "Oh, before I forget." I made my way to the bed and grabbed the twelve pack of beer from out of the box, set it on the counter. "For the first time, I feel like I'm contributing something to Loon Lake Inn."

She stored the extra beer in the fridge. Then she handed me the bottle of beer she'd already opened for me. It felt wonderfully cold in my hand.

"You see it too, huh?" she said. "Sonny is a little rough around the edges."

For the briefest of seconds, I pictured the stocky, round-faced man. His balding head, his stained apron, his crooked brown teeth. How the hell did a girl like Cora decide to marry a man like him? I guess it's like they say. Love is blind. But in her case, it was also more than a little messed up.

I stole a sip of beer.

"He treat you okay?" I asked, hoping I wasn't overstepping my bounds.

When she looked at me askew, I felt the fine hairs on the back of my neck stand up.

"Whatever do you mean, Kingsley?"

"I don't mean, does he hit you or anything," I explained. "I mean, does he treat a beautiful woman like you the way you should be treated?"

She grinned again, her face turning a distinct shade of red. "You mean like gold, Kingsley?" She gave me a wink.

I pursed my lips, and then drank some more beer.

"Now we're getting somewhere," I said.

But let's face it, it didn't take a genius to figure out that Cora was not exactly enthralled with Sonny. Let me take that back. She seemed to treat him okay. She wasn't openly hostile toward him. But for God's sake, she was way above his pay grade. She, on the other hand, could do a hell of a lot better. So what did that tell me? It told me that maybe he had something on her. Something that, if it were ever to get out, could make things very uncomfortable for her. Maybe even dangerous.

Or what the hell, maybe that was just my writer's imagination kicking into high gear. You know, me looking for a story. Any story.

"He seems like a tough guy, Cora," I said after a long beat. "Rough around the edges is an understatement. And you seem a lot more—"

"Charming. Sophisticated. Hot…" She took a couple of steps towards me in the already cramped cabin. She drank some beer, wiped her beautiful mouth with the tips of her manicured fingers. "How'm I doing, writer man?"

I felt my stomach cramp and my sex filled with precious blood. I might have even been blushing. I'd only just met this woman and, if I didn't know any better, she was coming on to me big time.

"Yeah," I said, my mouth suddenly dry, my pulse elevated just enough to make me slightly dizzy. "Something like that."

Time for me to drink some more beer, wet my way too dry whistle.

"Did you know that he was a criminal lawyer in his old life?" she said. "He's not as unwashed as you might think, Kingsley, despite that stained apron he wears in the kitchen."

She was so close to me now I could smell her sweet breath. It didn't smell like beer. It smelled like raw sex. Or maybe it wasn't her breath at all that I was smelling, but instead her pussy.

There, I said it. The P word.

When I first saw Cora, I couldn't help but think how much she looked like my wife. And what was the one thing I liked best about my wife? It wasn't her kindness, or her smarts, or her sensitivity. Because she possessed none of those things anymore. The thing I liked best was her pussy. I was drawn to it like a bee was drawn to honey. But therein lie the problem. Leslie was perfectly aware of how much I desired her pussy, and she used it against me like a weapon of war. She'd lock it away when she hated me, and on occasion, she'd unlock it and let me ravage it. Even then, she'd sometimes look at Netflix on her smartphone, or watch television, or even talk with a friend while I was going down on her. Didn't matter where I did it. In the bedroom, in the bathroom, in the kitchen, or in the living room, her legs spread on the couch and her black thong panties down by her ankles, I would go down on her until my jaw hurt. And when she decided she'd had enough and it was time to release, she'd let loose like Old Faithful. After that, she'd put her pussy back in the closet again for who knows how long. Just to make sure I couldn't get at it, she'd secure it with a padlock.

Ever since I went to the joint, I knew I had to find a replacement for Leslie's pussy. But this time it would be different. I needed to find a pussy that belonged to a woman who desired me as much as I desired her. This afternoon as I walked into the tavern, I knew right away I'd found that woman, and that it was just a matter of time until I not only got to her sex but until I got to her heart also. I didn't just desire a small piece of this woman. I wanted the whole package. I wanted her naked body, and I wanted her heart and her soul.

"Looks like Sonny's left the law far behind," I said after a time.

But I wasn't sure if I hated him more for knowing he was a lawyer once, or I just hated him because he had Cora to call his own and I didn't. Didn't matter, the result was the same. But then, who the hell was I to complain? She was coming on to me. I knew it, and she knew it. God knew it. So did the devil. For the briefest of seconds, I was convinced our lips were about to connect, and once that happened, there was no telling where it would all lead from there. Instead, Cora cleared her throat and took a step back. She drank down what was left of her beer and set the empty in the sink.

"I'd better be going," she said. "I'll leave you alone so that you can get settled."

My heart was throbbing in my chest. I wanted her so bad I couldn't stand it. My body was physically trembling with desire, and with a passion so profound my brain was buzzing and my sex was swelling. I wondered if she could see just how hard I was—if it was showing through my jeans. When I saw her eyes look me up and down, she couldn't help but see my hard-on. I wondered if it was turning her on. I could only hope so.

She made her way to the door.

"Listen," she said, "maybe, if you're not writing tomorrow, we can take one of the canoes out after breakfast and do a little fishing. The lake was just stocked and the brown trout are hitting like crazy. So are the bass."

"You're the first woman I've ever met who likes to fish," I said, knowing that Leslie would never go within ten feet of a fishing pole, much less touch a live trout. "You sure your husband won't mind?"

She placed her hand on the doorknob.

"So what if he does, Kingsley?" she said. "You're not afraid of him, are you?"

I felt my pulse elevate. Was she trying to get a rise out of me? She was succeeding at getting a rise out of more than just my heart rate.

"I'm a warrior," I said. "I don't scare so easy."

She licked her lips, making them moist and luscious. It was all I could do not to jump her, toss her on the table, and have my way with her, whether she liked it or not.

"You keep reminding yourself of that, Kingsley," she said. "Why don't you come by for dinner later at the tavern. It's our treat."

I wasn't sure how much I looked forward to having dinner with Sonny Torchi, but it was worth putting up with his presence so long as Cora was there.

"If you're sure it's no bother."

"I'll even toss in a few drinks," she said. "At Loon Lake Inn, peace and serenity is our motto."

Opening the door, I watched her walk out of the cabin and into my life.

6

Just to calm myself down, I opened a second bottle of beer and drank it down like nobody's business. God, it felt great drinking beer again. I'd lost my wife and daughter, but I'd gained a humble, lakeside chunk of the world. Or so it seemed. This morning I'd hocked Leslie's jewelry for cash, and now I had a nice cabin on a quiet lake in the Adirondacks with my own private beach. I had a job, and soon I'd be writing the novel that would pull me out of the bottoms. Yes, that's bottoms with an S. What more could a desperate ex-con want?

I went to the bunk, picked up the box of groceries, and brought them to the kitchen. I put everything away. Then I grabbed another beer and carried it down to the private beach. A cool wind was coming off the lake, and it caused ripples on the lake surface. In my head I saw myself back in uniform, my M16 gripped in both hands, tactical vest covering my torso, my 9mm strapped to my hip, my tan combat boots laced up tight. My scruffy face was grimy and gritty, and I peered at the blasted out two- and three-story concrete structures that flanked both sides of the street. Smashed concrete, broken glass, and twisted rebar were everywhere. My squad and I were being watched and targeted. It looked like we were entering a ghost town. Instead, we were being set up for an ambush. I whispered into my radio, "Wait for it…wait for it…" When the first RPG round came at us from a rooftop position maybe two hundred feet dead ahead, I knew we had a battle on our hands…

Welcome to Fallujah.

I drank some beer. I thought about the men I lost that day. Almost half the squad either KIA or shot up. One man lost a leg. Another, half his face. War was and remains hell. But damn if I didn't find something to love about it. Was it the exhilaration of surviving a rain of bullets and enemy explosives? Was it the hunt? The performing of duty in the face of constant fear? I never once thought I would die on the battlefield. I never contemplated having a leg or an arm blown off. I imagined what it would be like to have those things happen, but I never believed it could happen to me. And it never did.

Prison was a different story.

I was locked up in a big concrete and razor wire cage, and any number of bad things could have happened to me. From a shiv to the gut to a gang rape in the laundry facility to a bullwhipping in the shower room. The latter happened to me when I least expected it, but I damn well should have been expecting it. I'd let my guard down. The difference between the battlefield and prison is that in war, you had your brothers and sisters to rely on. They watched your back and you watched theirs. The Band of Brothers concept is most definitely not romantic bullshit. It is the truest of the true.

But in prison, it's every man and animal for itself. It was kill or be killed, if you'll pardon the cliché. But since I had no intention of being incarcerated for more than my allotted sentence, I most definitely stayed away from killing anyone for as long as humanly possible, even if they threatened me with my life, which happened on more than one occasion. I survived by keeping my eyes open even when I slept and by keeping my guard up at all times. The second you let your guard down is when the bad stuff happens.

It happened to me when a gang of Aryans, armed with strips of towels modified with metal shavings sewn into the ends so that they mimicked cat-o-nine-tails-like bullwhips, cornered me in the shower. I'd had a face full of soap and my eyes were shut. I never saw the first whip that connected with my back. But I felt the searing electric pain. It was so painful, it robbed me of my breath. Then came the second strike and a third. I felt my skin split open, the warm blood spray out. I dropped to my knees. I couldn't catch a breath. My eyes were burning from the soap. There must have been a half dozen of them, all of them armed with homemade bullwhips. They were striking me, rapid-fire, the pain so searing and bone deep, I felt myself going in and out of consciousness even before I hit the floor.

That's when somebody had the bright idea of turning the hot shower to cold. They sprayed the water down on me so that I wouldn't pass out. Then they whipped my body again and again. They whipped my back, my ass, my legs, my chest, my face. They cut me everywhere. Blood streamed into my mouth.

If only I could breathe, I might not feel so much pain…

No choice but to curl up in a fetal position, knees pressed against chest, face hidden between my thighs. I was a bloody mess. The cold water sprayed down on me, and I couldn't even work up the breath to scream. I was about to die, and they knew it. The last thing the Aryans wanted was a murder on their hands. What they wanted instead was a slave. They were terrorists who caught me in the weakest of moments.

They left me alone on the shower floor, my blood combining with the water as it was swallowed up by the drain. Only when my breath returned was I able to crawl out of the shower and onto the floor of gen pop, where a team of corrections officers found me. A general lockdown followed, and I was rushed to the prison infirmary where I remained in isolation for two months.

I drank more beer and gazed out onto the lake. A trout rose to the surface and caught a fly, then disappeared back into the lake. Natural selection at its finest.

I had my revenge on the Aryans. It was a quick affair and carried out with all the deadly efficiency of a midnight raid on a terrorist compound. Like I said, the prison superintendent had become a friend of sorts. We had a bond. We were brothers in arms. Brothers from another mother, despite the fact that I stood on one side of the bars and he stood on the other.

I'd also gained the trust of more than one CO. So when it came time for me to engage in payback for what those Aryans did to me in the showers, both the super and the COs had no problem turning their backs on what would surely be a massacre. The showers were once again the perfect place to carry out my mission. I waited until they were naked. Until one man knelt before the leader and took eleven inches into his mouth. While the other four swastika-tattooed men stood around, watching, jerking themselves off.

The shiv I carried had been fashioned from a plastic food tray one of the COs gifted me in exchange for a critique of the short story he'd just written. I was able to make an eight-inch razor-sharp knife from a long piece of that tray, the handle of which I wrapped in surgical tape lifted from the infirmary. That guaranteed an excellent grip even when it got soaked with blood, which it was sure to do.

I waited until the COs killed the lights per our pre-arranged agreement and only the red emergency lighting illuminated the big white devils. That's when I entered the shower fully clothed, my face hidden by a black kerchief, my head covered in a black skull cap. By then, I'd assumed full military mode, and I intended to put every bit of my lethal training to work.

I slit the first man's throat so fast he didn't realize he'd been cut. He just kept right on whacking himself off, until he began to choke on his own blood. Within a half second, I cut the second man. Then I quickly cut the throats on the third and fourth. As they dropped to the shower floor one by one, I wrapped my free arm around the kneeling man and slammed his jaw shut on the leader's cock. The leader screamed like a girl as I went to work on his kneeling lover's neck, opening it up like I was slaughtering an overly fat pig.

The blood that shot out of Leader's masticated dick was dark, nearly black in the dim red light. He was trying to stop the bleeding by pressing the pathetic folds of skin together, but all he was managing to do was paint his fat belly and meaty thighs in his own arterial blood.

When he dropped to his knees, I pulled down my mask and showed him my face.

"Remember me?" I said.

Then I pulled up my shirt and showed him my scars. Scars that were still thick and purple. His face drained of all its color. His mouth was opening and closing while the blood drained from his cut-off sex like filthy water pouring out of the ugliest fountain you ever did see.

"Got a present for you," I said.

Taking a knee on the blood and water soaked ceramic tile floor, I grabbed hold of his cut-off cock, pulled it out of his now dead lover's mouth.

"Open wide," I said to Leader.

He didn't respond. I pressed the blood-soaked business end of the knife against his throat. He opened his mouth. I shoved his own cock into his own mouth. Getting back up on my feet, I left him there to bleed out on his knees.

The bodies were taken away and incinerated. The

showers were cleaned up. As far as the superintendent and select COs were concerned, I'd been occupying my cell the entire night. I wasn't anywhere near the showers. They would attest to that fact should things get legal, which they never did. I'd provided the entire prison with a great service, and for that, I was never threatened nor touched again. I'd become something of a mythical figure to the rest of gen pop. A militarily trained vigilante killer.

It was something to be proud of. Trust me when I say, prison is no place for an altar boy.

Draining the rest of my beer, I headed back to the cabin and tossed the empty away. A quick glance at my watch told me the dinner hour was fast approaching. A shower, shave, and a clean shirt were in order. I wanted to look good for the caretakers of Loon Lake Inn.

Correction, I wanted to look good for the caretaker's wife.

7

By the time I made it to the tavern, Sonny was already seated at the bar, sipping on a cocktail. A martini. He was wearing a white button-down, a pair of black trousers over black loafers. He wore a gold chain around his neck, and his shirt was unbuttoned almost all the way down to his protruding gut. He slid off his stool when he saw me.

"You clean up okay, Kingsley," he said, going around the bar. "Hope you won't be too lonely out there in that cabin all by yourself."

Cora came immediately to mind. If she were to visit me every night for a while, I wouldn't be the least bit lonely.

"It's quiet," I said. "A good place to write. Thanks again for letting me take it."

Being that I was at the mercy of this man, I was trying to be polite and as kind as possible.

"Don't mention it," he said. "Like I already told you, you're gonna earn your keep."

He laughed when he said it, his voice doing that cracking and squeaking thing again. It was a horrible sound to have to put up with. But what the hell could I do about it?

"How about a drink?" he said. "It's all on the house tonight now that you're a brand new member of the Torchi team."

"You don't say," I said. "In that case, a cold beer and a Jameson back. Neat, if you don't mind."

"Don't mind at all," he said, turning and pulling the green translucent Jameson bottle off the top shelf.

"I'm a sucker for Irish whiskey," I said, just to make conversation.

He pulled a drinking glass out from under the bar back and poured a generous shot, then returned the bottle to the shelf. Grabbing one of the mugs set on a clean dishcloth, he drew me a beer from the tap, avoiding too much of a foamy head. Turned out Sonny was a pretty good bartender in his own right. But if I had to guess, I'd say he was an expert not at pouring for others, so much as pouring for himself.

He came back around the bar, sat back down on his stool. I sat down on the stool beside him. He lifted his glass as if to make a toast.

"So what shall we drink to, Kingsley?" he said, a smile painting his round, red face.

My eyes were gazing at him, but in all reality, they were searching for Cora. I couldn't stand being alone with him, and I wanted nothing more than for Cora to be in the room with us. Grabbing hold of my beer, I raised it up to his martini glass.

"How about your lovely wife, Cora?" I asked.

How could he object to a toast like that? But he chewed on it for a moment, as if even speaking about his wife was out of bounds. His round face went tighter, his dark eyes became beadier. But then he forced a grin. It told me he'd observed the way I'd been looking at her ever since I arrived this afternoon. He must have seen the effect she had on me. Maybe she had that kind of effect on lots of men, and it drove him mad.

But then there was the way she looked at me. There was the way she touched me. Touched my leg, the fingers on my hand, and my arm. If I didn't know any better, I'd say Cora had eyes for me also, and Sonny knew it. He clinked the rim of his glass to my beer mug.

"To Cora," he said, just the smallest hint of martini dripping over the rim.

"To Cora," I said.

We both drank. I downed a long swallow of the beer, then set the mug back on the bar. Lifting the drinking glass, I stole a sip of the whiskey and felt its wonderful burn. The burn hadn't yet abated when she waltzed into the tavern. Cora, looking lovely and happy in a short white dress that showed off smooth, milky legs that seemed to go all the way up to her shoulders. Her thick dark hair was pulled up into a bun, and her dress was wide open in the front, showing off a substantial amount of her cleavage and the black lace bra that had the privilege of holding her breasts. Like earlier, she wore a couple silver necklaces and maybe a half dozen silver bracelets on each wrist. But this time instead of cowboy boots, she wore gladiator sandals on her feet. Her toes had recently received a fresh pedicure and the nails were polished fire engine red. My favorite.

My heart beat hard in my chest and I felt myself growing excited. If only Sonny weren't seated beside me, I would have taken her in my arms and laid the most passionate kiss on her that I possibly could. I felt a slap on my arm.

"Earth to Kingsley," Sonny said. "You act like you ain't never seen a grown woman before, man."

If only he knew how long it had been since I'd seen a knockout like Cora. She approached us.

"Glad you could make it, Kingsley," she said, smiling shyly. "What are we drinking?"

Not only was she dressed beautifully, but she smelled

like lavender. If I closed my eyes, I was standing in a field of it, a cool breeze blowing on my face and Cora's hand in mine. We'd walk off into the sunset together. Sonny went to get up.

"Don't, Son," she said, heading around to the bar back. "I can help myself. You drink up."

She poured herself a glass of white wine and stood behind the bar in between us. I thought she might propose a toast, but she didn't. Instead, we drank for maybe a half hour, and we allowed the booze to sooth our nerves. I don't remember much of what we spoke about because all I could do was stare at Cora and imagine what it would be like to pull her dress off and fuck her on one of the tavern tables. At that point, I wouldn't have cared if Sonny joined in. That's how badly I wanted her.

A buzzer went off inside the kitchen and Sonny slipped off the stool.

"That would be the chicken," he said. "Dinner is about to be served."

He made his way through the kitchen door, leaving me alone with Cora. Correction, alone and happy.

For the longest time, I just stared into her deep, wet, brown eyes. In turn, she peered into mine from a couple feet away behind the bar. When she slowly came around the bar and slipped up onto Sonny's barstool, I couldn't help but notice the way her short dress rode all the way up on her thighs. So high, in fact, that her silky black panties were exposed. She couldn't help but notice me staring down at her angel space, and she quickly pulled down on the hem of her dress.

Heart be still.

"Guess I'm revealing more than a little leg," she said, not without a coy grin. She stole a sip of a newly poured glass of wine. "Oh, I needed that."

"Long day?" I said.

"Any day with Sonny is a long day," she said with a

66

roll of her eyes.

"You're in for a long, long life together," I said.

"Funny, Kingsley. Are your books that funny?"

"If you think murder is a laughing matter."

Her face went serious. "Murder is never a laughing matter," she said. "But I guess, in some cases, it can be justified."

Her words made my stomach go tight. What the hell did she mean by murder being justified sometimes? What the hell was Cora getting at? Maybe it was just her way of being provocative. As if her outfit and the body that filled it weren't already provocative enough. I was just about to ask her what she meant by the comment when the kitchen door opened and Sonny emerged with a tray in hand.

"Soup's on, people," he said.

Sliding off my stool, I took hold of Cora's hand and helped her down from hers. Her touch nearly took my breath away.

We seated ourselves at one of the round tables and devoured most of the roasted chicken which was served with roasted potatoes, ears of corn, and a fresh garden salad. Sonny might have been as unlikeable as they came, but I had to hand it to him, he was one hell of a cook. Of course, we washed everything down with more drinks. Lots of them. So many that Sonny was getting visibly drunk. His voice proceeded to get louder and louder, and he went on a jag about what a dump the town of Loon Lake was. How the hicks who lived in it had no vision. No ability to see beyond themselves and their pathetic, borderline poverty-stricken lives. Those hillbillies wouldn't know a dollar bill if it slapped them on the ass. Stuff like that.

Mostly, Cora just kept her head down, sipped her wine, and let him rant away like she was entirely used to his bullshit. I, more or less, did the same—just drank and listened.

I watched his round face get red and heated, observed the way he'd run his hand over his oil-slicked, receding hair when he wanted to make a point and how he spit his words the drunker he became. It was like a shooting gallery of Sonny's saliva spraying the table. It was disgusting and unnerving.

When he made a fist and slammed it down on the table, it was like a gunshot to the head.

"Goddammit!" he barked. "If only I could buy up this town and make it into a major tourist attraction. You know how many teenagers would fill the streets? Teenagers who want their pot, their crack, their smack, and their Molly? There's fucking money to make up here, Kingsley."

Drugs. Why the hell was he talking about drugs? Cora looked at me and cleared the frog from her throat.

"Sonny, darling," she said, "why don't you pull out your sax and play a song or two for us." Her eyes on me. "You'd like that, wouldn't you, Kingsley?" She winked when she said it.

I couldn't think of anything I'd rather not listen to than Sonny's saxophone. But then, if it meant I didn't have to listen to his banter, all the better.

"Why sure," I said. "I'd like that. Let's hear it, Sonny."

"What the hell," he said, smiling, pushing out his chair. When he got up, he was a bit unsteady, and he had to grab the chair back to balance himself. He tossed his now food-stained cloth napkin behind the bar, then made his way into the vestibule and the back office.

In the few seconds he was gone, I did something I shouldn't have. I reached out, took hold of Cora's hand, and squeezed it. She looked at me with wide eyes. She squeezed my hand in return, but then stole her hand back. I noticed then how the hem on her dress had shifted high up onto her thighs. Again, I could make out her black satin covered pussy. I swear she knew I was gazing at it, wanting it. Because she didn't adjust her dress. Not right away. If anything, I noticed how she opened her legs even more. When she ran her tongue over her thick lips, I thought I might faint.

Then, Sonny came barging back in, and she quickly crossed one leg over the other and pulled her dress back down as far as the hem could go.

"Whaddaya you guys want to hear?" Sonny asked, setting the saxophone case on the bar and opening it.

"How about a little Sinatra, dear," Cora suggested. "I just love it when you play Night and Day."

"Okay, baby," he said. "But first another drink."

He went around the bar, uncapped a bottle of Jack Daniels, and stole a deep swig right out of the bottle. Capping the bottle back up, he swayed his way back around the bar and took hold of his sax. Settling himself on one of the barstools, he placed the reed in his mouth, and he began to play.

It was Night and Day, just like Cora requested. I had to admit, Sonny wasn't all that bad a performer. Even for being drunk as a skunk, he was hitting all the notes with ease. But then, for some reason, he stopped.

"Come on, dance," he insisted. He waved his hand at us. "Come on now, don't just sit there. Dance."

Cora and I looked at each other. There was skepticism in her eyes, if not fear. I couldn't imagine that Sonny wanted me near his wife, so why, then, did he want me dancing with her? Dancing implied touching. Maybe he was trying to set me up. Trying to see if I might cop a feel. That would give him an excuse to toss me out on my ass.

"Dance, I tell you," he said. "Dance, or I'm not playing anymore."

"Oh, Sonny," Cora said. "We had too much dinner. I'm so full, I can't move."

"All the more reason to dance," he said. His voice was getting louder, more insistent. Angrier.

"If I fucking ask you to dance, Cora," he continued, "I mean I expect you to fucking dance."

Cora and I just went on gazing at one another from across the table. But that's when Sonny slipped off the stool, set his sax back down in its case. He trudged into the kitchen and came immediately back out with something in his hand.

It was a semi-automatic.

"Hey, Sonny," I said, feeling my heart beating against my sternum. "Take it easy, man. We'll dance if that's what you want. Isn't that right, Cora?"

For a time, our eyes locked. I saw not love or lust in her eyes. I saw real fear. Sonny was a loose cannon, that much was for sure. She slowly got up, pushed her chair aside.

"Come on, Kingsley," she said. "Let's dance."

I got up and went to her. I took hold of her hand and wrapped my arm around her trim waist.

"That's better," Sonny said as he placed his gun down on the bar and picked up his sax. "Get real close now. I like it when a handsome man presses up close against my woman."

So that was his game. He didn't like me touching or even breathing near Cora, but he must have gotten off on watching her with other men. Maybe not fucking other men, but simply dancing with them. It was his personal fetish—a man dancing with his wife at gunpoint. He wrapped his swollen lips around the sax reed and began to blow. The tavern once more filled with the sounds of Night and Day.

Maybe Sonny had a gun set on the bar only inches from his shooting hand, but the feel of Cora pressed against me was wonderful, like being in heaven. I was as hard as a rock, and I made sure she knew it by pressing myself against her. I stared into her eyes, and I sensed she felt every inch of me. She didn't try to avoid it either. If only I could just kiss her. But if I broke that barrier, it was an almost certainty that Sonny would drop the sax, pick up his gun, and aim the barrel at my head. He just wanted to watch his wife dance with another man and that's as far as it went. That was my guess anyway.

When the song ended, he placed the saxophone back in its case, and once again picked up his pistol, shoving the barrel into his pant waist.

"Show's over," he said. "Break it up, you two."

The Caretaker's Wife

He went back around the bar and helped himself to a generous shot of whiskey. He was so plastered now, he could hardly stand. Cora and I separated. But I could have held her like that forever. Didn't matter that Sonny had a gun.

"Sonny," she said, "I think it's time we called it a night, don't you?"

He issued her a grin that was filled with evil. It wasn't even a grin so much as a sneer. Who knows what goes on behind the closed bedroom doors of married couples, but if I had to guess, the experience wasn't a pleasant one for Cora.

"Do not tell me what to do, woman," Sonny said.

She glanced at me. It was as though she wanted me to do something.

"I'd better be going," I said. "It's been a long day, and I'd better get some rest if I'm going to be working the trails with you day after tomorrow, Sonny."

He laughed, high pitched and squeaky. It hurt my ears. "We're gonna put all those muscles to work," he said. He was slurring his words now.

"Thanks for your hospitality, folks," I said, heading for the door.

When I put my hand on the doorknob, Cora called out for me.

"Oh, Kingsley," she said. "I nearly forgot. You don't have any linens for the bed or towels for the bath. You go ahead, and I'll catch up."

I could hardly believe my ears. After everything that just happened, Cora was going to pay me a nighttime visit to my cabin.

Vincent Zandri

8

I made my way across the lawn and then took the trail through the trees back to the cabin. It was pitch dark under the tree canopy, and I had to take it slow or else walk face-first into a tree trunk. But when I made it through to the clearing, the full moon illuminated the little beach and the small piece of lawn leading up to the cabin. I started up the cabin steps, and something caught my eye. A trembling beam of white flashlight cutting through the darkness of the trees.

Cora.

I felt my heart lift.

"Just in time," I said.

"For what?" she said.

"A nightcap."

She was cradling a pile of linens and towels in her free arm while she held the flashlight in the other.

"God knows I need one," she said.

"You and me both," I said.

We headed inside the cabin, and she immediately

started on making up the lower bunk.

"Stop, Cora," I said. "You don't have to be my mother."

I laughed and pulled two cold beers out of the little fridge. I popped the tabs.

"I don't mind," she said. "Besides, you'll never get to it if I just leave the sheets there."

She was probably right. She made up the little bed and then placed the towels in the bathroom. I drank beer and watched her the entire time, the way her little white dress scooted up her milky thighs when she was tucking in the sheets, the way her breasts jiggled when she dropped the pillow into the pillowcase. The cabin was dimly lit but her big brown eyes shined.

When she was finished with her chores, she met me at the kitchen counter and took hold of her beer.

"Whiskey would be better," she said.

"Beggars," I said. "We can't be choosers."

"Let's take them outside. It's a beautiful night."

Sonny and his gun came to mind.

"What about your husband?" I said. "He's a crazy man tonight, if you'll beg my pardon."

"He's so drunk," she said, "he's already passed out on the bed." She exhaled. "Sorry you had to go through that, Kingsley."

"You sound used to it by now," I said.

"You have no idea," she said.

Outside, we sat on the porch step and stared out at the lake. The moonlight was shining over it, and every now and then a trout or a bass would jump and snatch a fly in mid-air. I was looking forward to fishing the lake tomorrow. I was looking more forward to spending time alone in a canoe with Cora.

We were silent for a time until she said, "When I was a girl, my family used to take me here. It was my favorite place on earth."

The Caretaker's Wife

"You used to come to Loon Lake Inn as a little kid?" I said.

She nodded. "How do you think I discovered it?" she said. "I lived in New York City where it was hot and grimy in the summers. That's why this place became such a beloved escape, for me and my whole family. We had a magical time in these cabins."

I thought about my own childhood. My stepfamily. I recalled the summers as hot and hard. We didn't vacation all that much. But I did plenty of work. Hard labor. Mowing lawns, digging ditches, gutting out old buildings. I got my first job when I was fourteen.

"I can see why you'd want to buy the place," I said.

"It had always been a dream of mine to own it," she said. "For as long as I can remember. I pictured myself retiring here with my children and grandchildren."

"You don't have any kids," I said. It was a question.

"Sonny can't," she said. "But I think it's more like he won't. Besides, I'm not sure I..."

She let the thought slide. But if I had to fill in the blanks, it would have been, "I'm not sure I would want to have a child with Sonny." I pictured him holding the gun on us. He was entirely unhinged, to say the least.

"What did you do before you became the caretakers of an inn?" I asked.

She drank some beer, gazed contemplatively out at the moonlit lake. But instead of answering my question, she stood and silently made her way back into the cabin. I could only assume she was setting her still full beer on the counter. When she came back out, she was gripping her flashlight.

I stood.

"Something I said, Cora?"

"It's late," she said.

In the light of the moon, I could see tears in her eyes. I reached out for her.

"No," she said. "I can't. Not now."

My heart sunk.

"Tomorrow," I said. "We'll take the canoe out."

She wiped both eyes with the backs of her hands. She worked up a smile.

"Yes," she said, turning on her flashlight. "Yes, we will. Goodnight, Kingsley. Sweet dreams."

"Good night, Cora," I said.

I watched her walk off into the trees.

I finished my beer and drank another. It was taking a little getting used to preparing myself for my first night not sleeping behind bars in nearly two years. When the beer was almost drained, I heard something that sounded like breaking glass. It wasn't a loud sound. It was faint, the trees muting most of the noise. I wasn't sure I would have even noticed it, had I not learned to notice the little things that go bump and crash in the night while I was in prison. Setting the beer on the table beside the typewriter, I went back outside.

Now I could hear voices. A scream that most definitely came from a woman, and following that, a shout that most definitely came from a man. Sonny. Sonny and Cora. I felt my way along the narrow trail that separated my cabin from the main cabins. When I came to the clearing, I could really hear them going at it.

Their apartment was located behind the office inside the Loon Lake tavern. I walked down toward the beach so that I could maybe get a look inside their windows. I had to do this without them seeing me.

Their bedroom was awash in lamplight. I could see Cora standing still, her arms crossed over her chest, her eyes wide and angry. Sonny was making fists with his hands, raising them in a threatening gesture. They were both screaming at one another. She yelled at him for pulling his gun, and he barked at her for flirting with, and I quote, "the new guy." Was he about to hit her? I couldn't be sure. But he was drunk enough to be capable of anything. A part of me wanted to barge in there and let him have it. But it wasn't my place.

I took a step toward the house and stepped on a stick. The stick was so dry it cracked under my boot. Sonny stopped shouting then. He went to the window and looked out onto the beach. I scooted out of sight. Whether or not I did this quickly enough was anybody's guess. But I knew it was high time I got the hell out of there before hothead Sonny came hunting for me with his gun. I headed for the trees and took it double-time back along the dark trail. I wasn't halfway to the cabin when I heard Sonny's voice shouting out into the night.

"Who's out here?" he barked. "I've got a gun, you hear me?"

I heard him loud and clear, that's for sure. Heading back inside the cabin, I shut the door and locked it. I finished my beer, drank one more, then laid myself down on the bunk bed. Compared to what I was forced to sleep on at Sing Sing, it was like sleeping on a cloud inside heaven itself. I went to sleep to the vision of Cora in my arms forever more.

9

"Well, top of the morning to you!" shouted a smiling and overly friendly Sonny Torchi as I came through the tavern door for breakfast. "How's that head of yours, Kingsley? You put down quite a few whiskeys last night, my new writer friend."

He was wearing a wife beater t-shirt three sizes too small for his gut. His hair was slicked back with gel, and he still hadn't shaved. Cora was setting a platter of scrambled eggs and bacon on the bar. She was freshly showered, dressed in her tight Levis and cowboy boots, a black button-down shirt tucked into her narrow waist. She was a sight to behold.

"Good morning, sleepy head," she said in that same innocent, happy voice she'd greeted me with yesterday.

Were these the same people who were fighting like cats and rabid dogs last night? Was this the same man who pulled a gun on us? Maybe Sonny was one of those guys who was a monster when he was drunk, but a jolly guy when he was stone cold sober. I had my doubts about the latter, but one thing was for sure, the food smelled good, and I was famished. Plus, I had to keep playing their game if I was going to live here for what essentially amounted to free.

"Help yourself, Kingsley," Cora said. "There's plenty. Orange juice and coffee are coming."

I thanked Cora and made a plate of toast, eggs, and bacon. I took the plate over to the same table where we'd eaten dinner last night. As I dug in, I shot a glance at Sonny. He must have already eaten because he sat down across from me with only a cup of black coffee.

"So, what are your plans for your day off, Kingsley?" he asked. "Better make it a relaxing day because I'll need you fresh for bartending duty tonight and trail clearing tomorrow."

"We're going fishing, honey," Cora said while setting a cup of coffee and a short glass of orange juice in front of me. She went to the bar, retrieved the milk and sugar and set those in front of me too. "We're going to catch some trout and maybe a largemouth bass or two."

"I love trout," Sonny said. "But you both better keep your eyes out for bear. I heard something rustling about last night, and I was convinced it had to be a bear. Sure enough, I got an email this morning from New York State DEC that said a tagged bear has been harassing residents of Loon Lake and also next door Paradox Lake. I can bet that's the bear I heard last night."

I felt a genuine sigh of relief that Sonny hadn't seen me outside his bedroom window. He got back up, went around the bar back, uncapped the bottle of Jack Daniels, and poured a generous shot into his coffee. He held the bottle up so I could see it.

"What about you, Kingsley?" he asked. "You want a sweetener for your coffee?"

I smiled. "Too early for me, boss," I said.

I thought maybe calling him boss from this point on might be a nice touch. Judging by the grin on his face, I could tell he liked it. He came back around and sat down.

"Maybe you should try to get some writing in today, Kingsley," he said. "You can write about a town that nobody ever heard of. A town nestled in the Adirondack Mountains. A town where the residents are poor souls who live on the edge of poverty and suffer through the worst bitter cold all winter long."

Cora sat down with a small plate of food. She took a bite, wiped her mouth with a napkin.

"Why would he want to write that, darling?" she asked.

"It would be realistic fiction," Sonny said. "True crime, if you ask me."

He drank some coffee, then got up again.

"Well," he said, "I gotta start on my sauce. Got some people coming for dinner later. They love their spaghetti and meatballs a la Sonny Torchi. I wouldn't want to disappoint them." He started for the kitchen, but then stopped just short of the door. He turned back around. "You two be careful out there. You won't be needing a chaperone, I hope."

When he belly laughed, I thought I might lose my breakfast.

"Don't be silly, darling," Cora said. "You're the only man for me."

"That's my girl," Sonny said, pushing the door open, and disappearing into the depths of the kitchen.

"Hurry up and eat," Cora said. "I want to get the hell out of here."

"Who can blame you?" I said.

I made a sandwich out of the eggs, bacon, and toast then downed my juice and coffee.

"All set," I said, standing.

Without uttering another word, we escaped the tavern for the peace of Loon Lake.

Cora had already outfitted one of the aluminum canoes with spinning rods and a cooler filled with cold beer and sandwiches. It meant a lot to me that she thought to take care of me like that. Leslie wouldn't be caught dead in a canoe on a lake with a fishing rod in her hand, much less think to fill a cooler with sandwiches and cold beer. It just wasn't in her makeup, her DNA. Her idea of a vacation was to go shopping in the same overpriced stores that she shopped in at home. Didn't matter if she was in New York City or Paris or right around the corner from Orchard Grove, she couldn't live without Nordstrom's, Macy's, or Tiffany's for even a day.

I quickly finished my breakfast sandwich, wishing I'd made another. Working together, we pushed the canoe into the water and got in, facing one another.

"There's a paddle for you," Cora said.

She picked up her own paddle and started paddling. "You paddle on the opposite side," she went on. "That way we'll keep her straight."

"Aye aye, captain," I said.

She laughed.

"I know a pretty good spot called Mary's Rock on the east side of the lake," she said. "It's also a beautiful view."

How do I explain how good I felt at that very moment in time? I was out of prison and free, and for the first time in a long time, I felt like my troubled past was behind me. I was sharing a canoe with a woman who I was falling in love with, and not even the memory of Leslie, Erin, or Theresa bothered me in the least. My life was all about living in the now. Enjoying every bit of the present. If anything was bothering me at all, it was knowing that Cora was married to a monster like Sonny. If only she were free of that man.

We came to a place where a huge granite boulder stuck out of the water. The rock looked like it was slowly emerging from out of the depths of the deep lake.

"Try your luck, Kingsley," she said, handing me one of the rods.

It had been a while since I last fished. But I'd done enough of it in the past to know how to use a spinning rod.

Pulling back on the reel release, I aimed the rod towards the rock and cast out towards it. The white rubber worm that was impaled onto the small hook landed maybe a few inches from the rock and quickly disappeared below the water's surface.

"Good cast," Cora observed.

"Aren't you going to fish?" I asked.

"I'd rather watch you for a while," she said.

I began to slowly reel in, picking up the slack, and feeling for any nibbles with my fingertips. When the fish struck, it took even me by surprise. The rod tip bent and bobbed and I felt the tension on the line.

"You've got one, Kingsley," Cora said excitedly.

"Damn," I said. "It's big whatever it is."

"Keep up the tension," she insisted. "But loosen the drag a little. That's only two-and-a-half-pound test."

Using my thumb, I released a little of the drag, and the fish took some line. If this was a trout, it was a damn big one. But when the fish broke the surface and jumped, I recognized exactly what it was—a big, largemouth bass. They must school all over the bottom of the rock formation. The fish gyrated and tried its best to throw the hook, but it couldn't. Cora let out an excited scream.

"That's a huge bass," she said. "Keep on him, Kingsley."

I kept up the tension, and kept reeling in, praying I didn't sever the line. After another minute or two of playing the fish, I could tell it was getting tired. I reeled in some more until the fish was right beside the canoe. Cora stuck her hand in the water and pulled the fish out by its mouth. Just like she'd said, it was a largemouth bass. It had to be six pounds if it was an ounce. It was long and thick with blue scales and a big white belly.

"That's a momma," Cora revealed. "Her belly is full of eggs. She needs to go back and repopulate the lake."

She gently pulled out the hook, and after taking another proud look at the fish, she set it back into the lake and allowed it to swim away. In a funny way, I felt like Cora had just saved a life. Maybe a lot of lives. So what if they weren't human? It showed me she had a heart.

"Toss out another cast," she said after a time. "Maybe you'll nail another."

I did as she told me and slowly reeled in. We were quiet for a time, while we relived the excitement of catching that huge bass over and over in our minds. But then I broke the quiet by asking about the rock.

"Why do they call it Mary's Rock?" I said.

Cora was holding her paddle and was busying herself with keeping the canoe in position so that we didn't drift too far away from the rock.

"A little girl named Mary drowned in this lake nearly a century ago," she said. "Some of the locals swear that on the anniversary of the night of her drowning, her ghost comes back to this rock. They say you can see her, wearing a little white dress and no shoes. Her hair is long and black, and her eyes are big and brown."

"Just like yours," I interjected.

"Mary sits on the rock, her knees tucked into her chest and she stares into the water like she's reliving her drowning, again and again."

I reeled in the worm and cast it back out again.

"That just might be the saddest story I've heard in a long time," I said. "How did she drown?"

"No one really knows. But they say it happened right around here. If she had lived, she'd be about one-hundred-twenty years old by now."

"And most definitely dead," I said.

Cora giggled. "I suppose you're right," she said. "Because no one lives forever, do they, Kingsley?"

I reeled the worm back in.

"No one lives forever, Cora," I said. "The point is to live the life you have."

She nodded. "Let's head somewhere else," she said. "I think that big bass you pulled in scared the rest of the fish off. I know some other really great places. Open a beer if you want."

I reached for my paddle when she reached for the cooler. It was entirely by accident, but our hands touched. Funny thing is, we didn't pull our hands back. Neither of us said, "Excuse me," or "Sorry." In fact, I not only didn't retrieve my hand, I took hold of hers and held it tightly. I felt my heart pounding in my chest, and my mouth went dry. What the hell was this? High school?

We just stared into one another's eyes while the canoe bobbed and the birds flew overhead. It was all I could do to prevent myself from pulling her to me and attacking her. But if I did that, we'd probably flip the canoe over. Maybe that would be a good thing. Something we'd laugh about later on. Was I becoming a hopeless romantic in my old age? There wasn't a whole lot of romance swimming around my brain right then. Instead, all I wanted was to ravage Cora. I wanted to attack her the way a hungry lion attacked raw meat. It was as much instinctual as it was primal.

"Who are you, Cora?" I said. "Where did you come from?"

"I could ask the same about you, Kingsley," she said.

Finally, she took her hand back. But that didn't stop my heart from pounding. My mouth had gone dry, so I opened a beer and drank down half of it in a single swallow. It was still morning, but I didn't care. I craved the calming effects of the alcohol. We proceeded to cover much of the lower lake's perimeter, the both of us casting out toward the shoreline. Cora used a fly rod at one point, casting it gracefully from the bow of the canoe. After a time, she caught a nice sized rainbow trout. She was so proud of it, she made me take a picture with her smartphone of her holding it in both her hands. Then she released it back into the lake.

"Won't Sonny want to grill that up?" I asked.

"I'd rather the fish live than Sonny carve it up," she said. "It's just too beautiful to be killed."

We fished and drank beer and ate sandwiches. As the afternoon wore on and the sun got higher, the fish stopped biting. We decided then to call it a day. We paddled back in, and Cora returned the cooler to the kitchen. I had to work at the tavern that late afternoon, so I thought I'd catch a quick nap. As I started to make my way back toward the trail that led to the cabin, Cora called out for me.

"Hey, Kingsley," she said. "Wait up."

I turned to see her running toward me, her lush dark hair bobbing against her shoulders, her eyes bright and beautiful. She caught up to me.

"Haven't you had enough of me today?" I said.

"I need to collect the towels you used for the laundry service," she said.

For some reason, I couldn't help but think it was an excuse for her to spend a little more time with me. Correction, a little more time with me away from her husband.

"The towels are still pretty clean," I said. "Bed sheets, too."

"Your idea of clean and mine are probably a lot different," she explained.

"It's your inn," I said.

"It's actually Sonny's," she said. "But I try to forget that."

Together, we walked the trail to my cabin.

The funny thing is, when we entered the cabin, she didn't collect any towels. Instead, she went to the refrigerator and pulled out a couple beers for us. We'd already been drinking all afternoon, so why stop now? Her face was tanned from the sun. We might have been fishing, but her skin still smelled like lavender. I wanted her so badly she had to have felt it even without me touching her.

She took a sip of her beer. I drank some of mine. I was feeling a bit tipsy, and I was certain she was too. I took a step closer toward her.

"Where are you from, Cora?" I asked. "Why won't you tell me?"

"Why is that so important to you, Kingsley?" she answered.

"Because I want to get to know you better. I want to know everything about you."

I came closer to her. She didn't back away. She merely drank some more beer, then set the can on the counter. I set my beer on the counter beside hers.

"You'll find out soon enough," she said, her voice now a tone deeper, sultrier. "That is, you hang around this place for a while."

I stepped even closer.

"I plan on being here for a while," I said.

She backed up then, slowly. Until her backside pressed against the table that held my typewriter and the stack of blank paper. I kept up with her, step for step. I closed more of the gap that separated us. When our lips were close to one another's, I couldn't help but connect with her mouth. I kissed her so hard, so violently, that my tooth cut her bottom lip. That might have frightened some women, but not Cora. She never stopped kissing me for even a New York second. She pressed herself harder into me, our tongues playing with one another despite the blood that seeped into our mouths.

She wrapped her hands around my head. I wrapped my arms around her waist. I yanked her to me so hard and so tight she couldn't escape my erection even if she wanted to. When we finally came up for air, I could see the little trickle of blood oozing out of her lip. I wiped it away.

"Do you want to stop?" I asked, my voice coming not from my voice box, but from somewhere deep down inside my soul.

"Shut up, Kingsley," she said, her voice no longer her own, but belonging to some woman entirely foreign to the school-girl-innocent woman who spoke with me on the phone yesterday and who later greeted me at the Loon Lake

Inn check-in counter. "Shut up and fuck me."

I began to unbutton her shirt, one by one. It was taking so long that by the time I got to the last two, I tore the shirt open and popped the buttons. Her breasts filled her black lace bra. Her nipples were hard. I pulled her bra down and cupped her left breast while suckling her right. She undid my belt, unbuttoned my jeans, and pulled my pants down, freeing my cock. That's when she dropped to her knees and took me in her mouth.

She began to suck me like she invented it. I swear, it had been so long since I'd had any physical contact with a woman, I was about to release in her mouth. How long could it possibly take when you haven't so much as breathed in the direction of a woman in twenty months' time? Not without a big pane of safety glass separating you, anyway. But I think she sensed I was about to come because she let go of me and said, "Not yet."

Standing, she unbuckled her belt, unbuttoned her jeans, and pulled them down. Her pussy was dark and trimmed to perfection. It was so wet it was glistening. I tossed her back on the table, spread her legs, and jammed my face into her succulent angel space, and I began to eat her until I worked her up into a creamy froth. She was moaning and gyrating her hips. She used both her hands to pull on the back of my head as if she wanted my entire head inside her pussy. And I wanted nothing more than to be inside her pussy. I wanted my whole body engulfed by her warm wetness and pink, hot flesh.

"Fuck me, Kingsley," she begged. "Fuck me now, you son of a bitch."

I wasn't about to disappoint her. I wasn't about to disobey her either. Backing away from her, I stood and grabbed hold of her legs and dragged her toward me. When I slipped my cock inside her, I thought my skin was on fire. That's how hot she was. That's how wet she was, her juices boiling like she hadn't had sex in years. And maybe she hadn't.

I tried to go slow, going harder and harder with each thrust. I knew it hurt, but I think she liked it that way. I think she liked the pain. She wanted the pain the same way a vampire wants fresh blood.

I felt myself filling up until I knew I couldn't hold it any longer, and I knew she was coming to that same place.

"Come in me," she pleaded. "Come in me. Come in me, you bastard."

I couldn't possibly hold it any longer. When I released, so did she. Our screams had to have been heard outside the cabin. Christ, they could have been heard all the way up at the Canadian border. But we didn't care. For those few beautiful seconds when she was me and I was her, we didn't care who the hell heard us, so long as we were as one.

When we were done, I stood back, a bit off balance, but happier than I had been in months. Fuck that. Happier than I had been in years. I could taste her blood on my tongue and her pussy on my lips, and I knew she could still feel me inside of her. With every movement she made sliding off that table, she could feel my juices swimming around in her. I was a part of her now. She was a part of me. Now we would have something that would be ours and ours alone. Something that did not belong to Sonny.

Pulling up my pants, I went to kiss her again. But she pushed me away.

"Don't," she said.

Her mood had shifted one hundred-eighty-degrees.

"Something I said, baby?"

"Just don't," she said, getting quickly dressed.

A man's voice could be heard outside the cabin walls. "Cora," the man barked. "Cora, where the hell are you?" I'll be damned if it wasn't Sonny.

10

My heart shot up into my throat. I locked eyes on Cora. She didn't seem the least bit fazed. As though her husband intruding on her while she was mopping up after a particularly good lay was an everyday occurrence for her.

"Jesus," I said, "I think he heard us."

"Relax, Kingsley," she said, tucking in her shirt, buttoning the few buttons she had left. "Sonny is blind to everything but what he wants to see."

I buckled my belt. I thought about what just happened. The sex. If I were writing this as a novel, I would never have it happen so fast. I would have my character hang around the inn for at least a few weeks, let the tension build between him and Cora. But that's not the way it was meant to be. Like me, she must have known from the moment she saw me that she wanted to fuck me.

"What about the beers?" I asked, nodding in the direction of the kitchen counter.

"So, we're having a beer," she said. "What of it? We've

been fishing all afternoon. Goes with the territory."

She went to the counter, took hold of hers, and drank, as casually as if she were back at the tavern. Footsteps on the small porch outside the front door. Then the front door opening. Sonny stepped in, a big grin painting his face.

"Figured I'd find you two here," he said. He looked around a little. Then, "So, how you like your new digs, Kingsley?"

He wasn't wearing his stained apron, and because of it, his belly was more pronounced, his chest more barrel shaped. His button-down work shirt was sweaty under the armpits, and there was a tear in the left side so that a portion of his graying undershirt was exposed. I couldn't explain it exactly, but just the sight of that dirty, sweat-soaked undershirt made me nauseous. Like he wasn't a living, breathing human being, but instead, a rotting carcass. What the hell, maybe he was a zombie.

"The cabin is just fine, Sonny," I said. "Can't thank you enough for everything."

He glanced at the typewriter which by now had been pushed to the very edge of the table. We all focused on it as if it were wrapped in flashing red neon. Half of it was hanging over the side. It would take just the slightest breeze to make it fall off the table. If that happened, I couldn't afford to buy another. Also, the ream of white paper was no longer neatly stacked but instead, looked like an unshuffled deck of playing cards.

Cora quickly reached out for the typewriter, pushed it back into the center of the small table. She also quickly straightened out the paper. I looked into Sonny's eyes. They shifted to one of the chairs that had been pushed away from the table. He picked it up by its back and set it under the table where it belonged.

"Damn," he said, not without a guttural laugh. "Beers, tossed furniture, and a typewriter nearly thrown to the floor." He squinted his eyes at Cora. "And what happened to your lip, Cora?"

"I bit it after I landed a nice rainbow trout," she said. "You know how I get when I get excited."

Sonny laughed. "Yeah, I know how you get when you get excited all right." Looking around the cabin again. "I didn't know any better, I'd say you two were having a nice little private party."

I was pretty good at hiding any signs of my emotions by now. In prison, you learned how to make a face of stone and keep it that way. You never wanted to look too happy—easy—but you also never wanted to look too sad or angry—not easy. Facial expressions attracted attention. Not only from the bullies who wanted nothing more than to mess you up just for the fun of it, but also from the COs who liked to pick on you almost as much. The golden rule was to maintain the best poker face possible, and never—and I mean never—look anyone in the eye.

It was exactly the kind of thing I had going here. Sonny wasn't dumb. That is, he truly was a criminal lawyer. He must have had some sort of nose for sniffing out shit when it was going down. It wouldn't take an Einstein to know that something strange had just happened inside the cabin. Christ, the place smelled like pussy. And when his bloodshot eyes shifted their focus one more time to something that was lying on the floor, I thought for sure that Cora and I were beyond screwed.

He bent over, retrieved my wallet. For a long beat or two, he just held the old, worn leather wallet in his hand, turning it this way and that like he'd just discovered a priceless ancient relic. He stuffed his tongue in his cheek, and it bulged out like a tumor.

"This, ummm, yours, Kingsley?" he asked.

For the briefest of seconds, I scanned the floor, making sure Cora hadn't left her panties lying around. A typewriter hanging precariously off the edge of the table was one thing. A chair that was set askew was another. Even finding my wallet on the floor could somehow be explained. But if his wife's precious undergarments should just happen to be lying about, it would spell disaster for Cora and me.

"What's the matter with you, Kingsley?" Cora broke in, her beer can still in hand. She'd worked up the same kind of aggressive smile she had when I first hooked into the largemouth bass. "You'd forget your head if it wasn't attached."

Sonny snorted. He handed me back the wallet. "What we have here, Cora," he said, "is the intellectual type. Always living inside his own head, oblivious to the outside world. Now, isn't that right, Kingsley?" He slapped me on the shoulder. His hand was so thick and hard, it felt like a sledgehammer. He nearly knocked me off my feet. "Well, all that's gonna change now that we're about to put you to work." He reached into his pocket. "Anyways, I came out here not to chat it up but to give you the key to the bar cash register." Reaching into his opposite pocket, he pulled out a wad of cash. "Here's two-hundred cash, Kingsley. Use it to make change. I want all receipts, so I have a full accounting of where the money is going. Not that I don't trust you."

He handed me the key and the cash.

Cora finished her beer. Chugged it, was more like it.

"Darling," she said, heading to the kitchen and depositing the empty into the trash can, "I'm sure Kingsley is not the devious type. You know how I've always had a good instinct for judging character, and I believe what we have here is a real gem. Not a bad fisherman either."

So, that was it, then. Cora had made her pitch to her husband. She'd vouched for my character almost as good as my lawyer did for the parole board, and she didn't know me inside and out like he did. Nor did I know her. But the truth of the matter was that Cora had fallen for me as hard as I had fallen for her. Considering the proximity of her husband, I wasn't sure if that was good luck or the worst luck a man could have.

"The tavern is closed for now, Kingsley," Sonny said, turning for the door. "But make sure the door is open no later than six. Those trout fishermen get mighty thirsty after a day on the water. And don't lose that cash, you hear me?"

As he set his hand on the doorknob, I noticed something bulging out of his waist where the tail of his work shirt had come out. As he opened the door, the shirttail shifted, and the grip on a small pistol was exposed. The sight of the gun sent a noticeable chill up and down my spine. Sonny was packing. Not an unusual thing up in these parts where a bear could suddenly appear out of nowhere. But knowing that he had pointed that same gun at Cora and me last night not only gave me pause, it told me Sonny was a dangerous man, sober and drunk.

He opened the door and stepped out.

"Coming, Cora, my love?" he barked.

"I gotta go," she whispered.

That's when she did something she shouldn't have. By that I mean she was taking a real chance when she snuck a lightning fast peck on my cheek. We were facing Sonny's back, but that didn't mean he did not have a pair of eyes in the back of his pumpkin head.

"He's dead to us," she whispered in my ear. "Do you understand me, Kingsley? He's a monster, and I want him dead." Then, composing herself, "Coming, honey!"

I didn't breathe until she closed the door behind her.

I immediately went to my bag, pulled out my old laptop, set it up on the table beside the typewriter and the ream of paper. It was time to do a little detecting on exactly who Cora Black and Sonny Torchi were. What their past lives were and how and why they settled on the isolation of Loon Lake. Something aside from the fact that Cora might have vacationed here as a child.

Powering up the laptop, I clicked on the little icon at the bottom of the screen that would direct me to an open Wi-

Fi network. Turned out, there weren't any networks. I was too far north where the internet was still something that wasn't always available. Talk about rustic. Talk about isolated.

I closed the laptop lid, sat back in my chair. My mind was spinning and my body still trembling from the sex I had with Cora. Only yesterday morning, I boarded a Greyhound bus at dawn for the hour and a half trip back up to Albany. Maybe I hadn't been hearing from them much anymore, but my wife and daughter knew I was coming home. They knew it, and I fully expected them to be waiting for me at the front door with open arms. Okay, maybe not open arms, but they might have greeted me with a smile and just a few simple words like, "It's good to have you home again, Daddy." Instead, all I got was an empty house, my clothes and damaged typewriter stuffed into a box and tossed carelessly in the garage to rot. I was lucky to get my laptop and Jeep back.

There was nothing left for me in that house, so I came here to Loon Lake Inn. It was as if I was drawn here the entire time not by necessity, but by fate. I met a woman, Cora, who not only reminded me of Leslie, physically speaking, but I began to fall in love with her hard. It was love and lust at very first sight. Again, only fate could make something like that happen. We weren't in one another's company for more than twenty-four hours before we're screwing like two college kids right on the table in the little cabin. A cabin that would be home for me for who knows how long.

Then there was the issue of Sonny. Good old violent, pistol-packing Sonny. He was good with me staying here for free, but free wasn't really free since he expected me to work.

Tending bar wouldn't be much of a hassle. Like I said, it was my way of getting free booze. Plus, there might be a chance to skim a little off the top, depending on the day's take. Bartending was a cash business, and I'd done plenty of it when I was in college to make ends meet. Skimming off the top was what made it so lucrative for bartenders who knew what they were doing. But my work wouldn't end there. Sonny was insisting on getting some physical labor out of me. Tomorrow, I'd meet him at dawn to clear the trails. My gut told me he was really going to bust my hump and enjoy it.

"He's dead to us. Do you understand me, Kingsley?"

Maybe Cora was right. If only Sonny were out of the picture. If only he were gone. Dead and gone. Cora and I could live up here in this idyllic place and be happy forever after. I kept hearing her words over and over again inside my head like a broken record. "He's dead to us." There was only one explanation for that. She wanted him gone as much as I did. Maybe she didn't come right out and say it. But Cora wanted me to help make it happen.

She wanted me to commit murder for her. For her and me.

I glanced at my watch. I had an hour and a half until I was expected to be at the bar slinging drinks. Maybe I should try to get some writing done, or so I thought. But I couldn't have come up with a creative thought right then if it slapped me over the head. For the hell of it, I pulled out my smartphone, which by now was old and no longer so smart. The screen had cracked over the time I was in the joint, which told me whoever was taking care of it inside prison storage had dropped it, maybe by accident or maybe on purpose. Prison employees, especially COs, could be real assholes if they wanted to be.

Pressing the Google app, I started typing in Cora's name. Maybe the cellphone provider would allow me access to the internet. But just like my laptop, the system told me no network was available. You just couldn't fight the fact that you were in the deep woods and off the grid. It made me feel good on one hand to be so lost, and sort of sad on the other.

My eyes locked on the phone and its numerous apps. I knew I shouldn't go there, but I pressed the photo app icon. I shuffled through the pictures until I came to a series of snapshots I took of Leslie and Erin on the beach in Cape Cod three or so years back. They both looked so happy. Erin in her little blue and white bikini and Leslie in her sleek fitting black one piece. We'd purchased a fire engine red blowup swan for Erin, and she was floating around in the shallow end of the water with it, while Leslie looked on anxiously. Even now—now that she'd left me—my stunning wife took my breath away. Tall, tan, fit, her long dark hair draping her shoulders, her big brown eyes masked by aviator sunglasses. I remembered thinking I would rather die than let anything bad happen to her or our daughter. They were my everything, and for a long time, I was only too happy to give them everything they wanted.

Funny, because the pictures were taken at the very same time the bathroom renovations were happening at the house. We scheduled the trip so the carpenter could have the run of the place while we were gone. Little did I know, Leslie must have been texting him while we were hanging out on the beach, soaking in the sun while our daughter played in the waves with her red blow up swan…while I felt the happiest I had ever felt in my life.

Maybe I'd made a mistake after all. Maybe when I tossed that carpenter out the window at Lucy's Bar, I should have completed the job I'd started when I was pounding his head against the pavement. Maybe, in the end, I should have bashed his brains in even if it meant a life sentence. Maybe it would have been worth it. At the very least, I should have taken Theresa up on her offer of being lovers when I had the chance. But I wanted to be loyal to Leslie. I wanted to be true to her. What a fool I was.

My eyes were filling. My mouth went dry, and my stomach cramped. I had to get my head straight and lose the bad thoughts that were poisoning my brain. That meant only one thing. I needed to take some action or else I would drink that refrigerator dry before I was expected to show up at the Loon Lake Inn tavern to tend bar.

The Caretaker's Wife

Getting up, I grabbed my keys and my laptop. I left the cabin and took the trail back to the main lodge parking lot. I got back in my Jeep, fired her up, and before Cora or Sonny could stop me, I drove out to the main road and headed for town.

I was on a mission to find some Wi-Fi and find out the true identities behind the caretaker and the caretaker's wife.

Vincent Zandri

11

Loon Lake wasn't much of a town by any stretch of the imagination. It consisted of one main street flanked by maybe a dozen buildings. I passed by a couple of sad looking single-story commercial buildings, a hardware store, and a funeral parlor. A few two-story homes were located on the road. One of them was so badly burned it was uninhabitable. Long strips of yellow crime scene ribbon had been draped around what was once the front door.

A bar occupied the lot beside a small grocery store that also housed a small diner and some gas pumps outside. A beat-up sign that barely hung from a rusted post announced, Bunny's Place. Across the street was a combination post office, sheriff's headquarters, fire station-slash-EMT brigade, and a jail. Two prowlers were parked out front along with a white pickup truck. Across the street was a two-story brick building that housed an insurance business. Chuck Dreadgold — Insurance Agent read the sign outside.

Further down the road was a library and beyond that

a white wood clapboard church. A few more mixed-use buildings occupied the street, but not much else. From where I stood after I parked the Jeep in the lot outside Bunny's Place, there wasn't even a decent restaurant in town. But maybe that was good news for the Loon Lake Inn tavern.

My laptop under my arm, I entered into the bar. It was a small, one-room affair with a pool table to the left and a couple of booths to the right. The bar was in the back of the room across from the toilets. A flat screen TV mounted to the far wall was broadcasting hockey. I wasn't much into the sport, but I knew that men and women up here loved it. Hockey was a cold weather sport, and it was teeth-chattering cold up here three quarters of the year.

The woman tending bar had to be about my age. She was small, but wiry in her CBGB black t-shirt, the short sleeves rolled up like she enjoyed showing off her biceps. Her hair was black, probably a dye job, and her eyes weren't wide so much as overly charged. They gave me the impression she wasn't just naturally high on life, but on some sort of chemical speed. Crack maybe. Or crystal meth. When she smiled, she was missing a bottom tooth.

I set my laptop down on the bar.

"You Bunny?" I said.

"That's me," she said. "What ya drinking?"

"Irish whiskey if you got it," I said.

"We ain't all hicks up here," she said.

I opened the laptop while she grabbed the bottle off the shelf behind her. The machine was already powered up since I hadn't turned it off inside the cabin. I clicked on the Wi-Fi icon.

"You got internet, Bunny?" I said.

"Told you we ain't all hicks," she said, pouring me a generous shot of whiskey.

"Password?" I pushed.

"Sensei one oh one," she said. "No spaces."

"Sensei," I said. "As in karate sensei?"

"Yup," she said. "You don't think this joint makes me any money, do you? I'm a fourth-degree black belt. Teach at a dojo over in Crown Point everyday 'cept Sundays and Mondays. Late afternoons, I open this joint. Keep it open until a fight breaks out and I gotta break somebody's head. Usually a biker."

"If you're not making dough, then why keep it open?"

"Public service," she said.

"Very thoughtful of you, Bunny."

I took a good look at her. Was this woman truly capable of pounding on a big ass biker? She couldn't have stood more than five foot four. If she was one-hundred-twenty pounds wet, I'd be shocked. But then again, she was in good shape, and I knew from prison experience it wasn't the size of the dog in the fight, it was the size of the fight in the dog. I'd seen more than one little skinny white dude make hamburger out of some six foot six black stud's face when sufficiently provoked.

I sipped the whiskey and typed in the password. It worked. I finally had a connection to Google. First things first. I typed in the name Cora Black. I knew there couldn't be many women in the world with that name, so the information that came up had to belong to my Cora Black. Not many things shock me anymore, but Cora Black's Google profile certainly did.

Case in point...

First item that appeared was a New York Post headline from way down in Manhattan. Cop Busted in Sex Ring. I might not have believed what I was seeing had the accompanying picture not been Cora's pretty face.

"No wonder she wouldn't answer me about her past," I whispered to myself.

My pulse picked up speed, and I felt a strange chill in my gut. I drank some more whiskey to fight it. I gave the article the once over. It went on about how Cora, along with some of the new young male and female recruits, were getting together on weekends and, well, getting it on. When a digital video of one of the sex parties emerged, the NYPD IG got involved and swiftly shut the party down. Cora was handed her pink slip minus her pension which, by then, was substantial. And the lawyer she hired to help get her out of the mess? You guessed it. Sonny Torchi.

Bunny cleared her throat.

"Holy crap, pal," she said. "You look like you just saw your own ghost."

I guess my facial expression must have been betraying me after all. That and the fact that my face must have gone noticeably pale. What can I say? It happens. Nothing can prepare you for the fact that the woman you've just fallen head over heels for was once involved in a sex ring with men and women years younger than her. Don't get me wrong, I didn't expect Cora to be Snow White any more than I'm Prince fucking Charming. Who the hell is? It's just that I was having trouble equating the sweet young thing who operated the Loon Lake Inn check-in counter with the woman in the New York Post photograph—the very woman who was attempting to hide her face with both her hands, but failing miserably.

But then, wait one second here. Why the hell had I been so surprised to find out Cora was no saint? Didn't she just fuck me to death on the table inside my cabin? Didn't she just tell me to my face that she wanted her husband dead?

And didn't she do it in a way that suggested she wanted me to help her make it happen?

There was another reason not to jump to conclusions. If Cora had wanted to hide her past, she would have changed her name. My guess is, she made a mistake, paid for it, and moved on. Nothing wrong with that. But now she owed Sonny her life, and there was something definitely wrong with that.

I drank down the whiskey.

"Another, Bunny," I said.

"Jeez," she said, "you must be having a rough day."

104

"I just got out of the joint," I said.

She poured my drink and gave me a slant-eyed look that suggested she thought I was messing with her.

"What's your name?" she said.

I told her.

"Where've I heard that name before?"

"I used to write novels."

Her eyes lit up.

"That's it," she said, pointing her finger at me. "You're that writer who fucked up that big guy down in Albany. Guy who was messing around with your wife. I remember you from the news. You really took it to the asshole, didn't you? Tossed him through a window, punched the daylights out of him. You're one tough son of a bitch, mister."

Okay, I couldn't help but be more than a little pleased with myself.

"Well, I'm trying to keep out of trouble now," I said.

"How long you in town?"

"Long enough to write a novel."

"Where you staying?"

"Loon Lake Inn," I said. "You know it?"

Her face went tight. She leaned in over the bar closer to me, as if we weren't the only one's occupying the joint.

"You be careful of them," she said.

"Of who?" I said.

"You know," she said. "Cora and her husband, Sonny. Since they moved in, everything has changed. People are afraid of them."

I shook my head.

"Why?"

She looked over one shoulder and then the other. "Torchi is no one to mess with," she said. "He and his family down in New York City are trying to buy up the whole town and doing it for pennies."

I sipped my drink, tried to digest what she was telling me. I remembered a drunken Sonny going on and on last night about how the residents of Loon Lake wouldn't know a dollar bill if it slapped them on the backside. How they had no vision for the future. How they preferred poverty to posterity.

I typed the name Sonny Torchi into the laptop search engine. Several articles about his work as a defense lawyer popped up, including one article about how he saved Cora's pension when she was forced to retire from the force. Scanning the article, the author suggested Torchi used the power behind his extended family to make it happen. The lawyer made the judge an offer the court could not possibly refuse.

"Either that or he ends up with a horse head in his bed," I mumbled.

"What?" Bunny said.

I shook my head, closed the laptop lid.

"Just talking to myself."

Just then, the silence of the peaceful little town was shattered by the roar of engines. Motorcycle engines. Harleys if I had to make a guess.

"Oh shit," Bunny said. "Here they come."

"Here who comes?"

"Torchi's men," she said, not without a sad smile. "Don't you see what's going on here, Mr. Kingsley? Sonny Torchi is holding this town hostage."

The bikers pulled into the parking lot and killed their engines. Bunny and I watched them from the front picture window. There were three of them. They were all pro-football lineman huge and dressed in black leather. Their motorcycles were Harleys, just like I thought. I didn't know much about motorcycles, but I knew Harleys were expensive. As they started for the door, Bunny's face lost all its color, and she made her way fast back behind the bar, as though having it between she and them made all the difference in the world. It was a strange move for a woman who was a black belt and who bragged about pounding biker's heads together.

It made me a little nervous. But then, I wasn't exactly afraid either. I'd survived the bloody fight for Fallujah, and one of the most dangerous maximum security prisons in the country had been my home for a long time. Facing down goons like Torchi's men was a twenty-four seven experience for me.

I was more curious than anything else. I went to the pool table and decided to toss a couple quarters in the slot that released the balls. As the front door opened, I was wracking the balls. All three men walked in. Two of them hung back near the door while one of them, a man who was so big he seemed to fill up the entire bar, made his way toward Bunny.

"How's my favorite toothless bartender?" Big Man barked.

One eye on Big Man, the second eye on the other two, I shoved the plastic wrack under the table, grabbed a pool cue off the wall, and lined up the white cue ball, readying myself for the break. The two big goons behind me were watching me. It wasn't so much that I could feel their stares digging into my back, I could see them with the eyes I'd grown in the back of my head. Taking careful aim, I broke the triangular stack like I meant it. The gunshot-like collision of the break was enough to grab the attention of Big Man.

He turned.

"Who the hell are you?" he said.

For the first time since they walked in, I felt a start in my heart. Gazing quickly at Bunny, I could see she was trying to pass on a message to me. Her wide, unblinking eyes told me to mind my own business. But I had been minding my own business. More or less. Still, the man asked a question, and even though I could see he was a big asshole, I thought he deserved a proper retort.

I looked over one shoulder and then the other.

"You talking to me, sir?"

I knew from experience that the sir part would be

a nice touch. Big assholes like him always ate up pseudo respect like a sponge soaks up water.

"Yeah, I'm talking to you," he said. "I've never seen you here. And it's too early for the two or three tourists this pathetic backwater town gets in the warm weather."

"He's just passing through," Bunny said.

He shifted his eyes back to her quick.

"I wasn't talking to you, Bunny."

"Let's just say I like sleepy little towns," I said.

I continued to sink ball after ball.

"Now then, Bunny," Big Man went on, "it's that time of the month. And I don't mean between your legs."

So, that was it, then. He was looking for a payout, and he wasn't the least bit afraid to demand it in front of me. That was another thing I'd gotten used to in the joint. Screws expecting payouts from inmates, inmates expecting payouts from screws, and inmates expecting payouts from other inmates. Payment could be in the form of blowjobs, drugs, or even good old-fashioned cash. But the principle was the same. You owed somebody, for whatever reason, you'd better make the payment or else face some pretty bad shit. That's exactly what we had going on here.

I hit another ball into a side pocket. Turning, I smiled proudly at the two silent goons. They didn't smile back.

"I'm a little short this month, Billy," Bunny said. "Like you said, tourists ain't arrived yet."

Big man shook his head slowly. Maybe even dramatically, if you know what I mean. Sort of like a parent would do to a kid when they got caught raiding the cookie jar before dinner.

"Now, now, Bunny," he said. "I thought we had an agreement."

"I ain't got no agreement with you, Billy," she said, her voice getting louder, tone more agitated. "I don't make no deals with nobody. It's that sneaky Sonny Torchi who makes the one-sided deals."

Big Billy made a fist, slammed it down on the bar. The entire bar rattled.

Another glance at the goons behind me. They were smiling now, like watching Billy lose his shit was the most fun they could have with their leather on. I sank another ball into the corner pocket. Did it just to make it look like I wasn't the least bit fazed by the big asshole's tantrum.

"It's only four-hundred bucks, Bunny," he said. "Now, I'm sure you can spare four-hundred bucks. You make that in tips alone on a Saturday night. Or do I have to open up the register for you?"

Bunny crossed her arms tight around her chest.

"I told you already," she said. "I don't have it. All I got is the cash that man over there is paying for his drinks."

Suddenly, all eyes were on me. I sank one last ball, then stood up straight. Setting the cue onto the tabletop, I slowly made my way back to the bar. Taking hold of my whiskey, I drank it down in one swift pull. Then I set the glass back down.

"One more, Bunny," I said, "if you're not too busy."

Big Billy cleared his throat like he was trying to get my attention. An elephant could have been standing beside me and he wouldn't have been more obvious. And trust me when I tell you, Billy was as big as an elephant. He moved in toward me, leaned down so that he could talk into my ear.

"Case you hadn't noticed, friend," he said, "I'm presently engaged in a little conversation with the proprietor of this dump."

Snickers from the rat pack by the door. My guess was they got chewed out if they didn't laugh at the boss's jokes. Bunny grabbed the bottle of Jameson. For a long beat, I just stared into the drink. Until I raised the glass and pulled it back in one swift swallow.

Setting the glass back down hard, I said, "How much I owe you, Bunny?"

"Fifteen," she said.

I pulled Sonny Torchi's money and what was left of my money from out of my pocket, peeled off a ten and a five, slapped it down on the bar.

Then I said, "Oh, Bunny, I almost forgot the tip."

I laid out the rest of the cash I had on hand, including Torchi's tavern money. It wasn't four-hundred, but maybe it was enough to satisfy Big Billy in the short term. Bunny looked at me with eyes wide open. She offered me just a hint of a grin, but its meaning was huge. She was thanking me from the bottom of her heart. Peeling the money off the bar, she counted it out loud and swiftly handed it over to Big Billy.

"Satisfied?" she said. "I'll have to owe you the extra fifty."

He folded the money without bothering to recount it, and stuffed it in his vest pocket. Then he went behind the bar, opened the bottle of Jack Daniels that was sitting on the top shelf. He downed a generous shot. He set the bottle back without capping it and wiped his lips with the back of his hand. When he came back around the bar, he turned to me, said, "You think you're pretty smart, don't you, friend?"

"Comedy was never my strong suit," I said. "I like to take life seriously. Don't you?"

"Watch your fucking mouth, jerk," one of the peanut gallery goons said. He was wearing leather chaps and a leather vest over a black t-shirt, just like the other one. He was even bigger than his boss, if such a thing were possible.

"I've got this, PJ," Big Billy said.

That's when Big Billy poked me in the ribs with an extended index finger. Normally, a finger poke didn't hurt, but coming from a dude his size, I felt it all the way down to the bone.

"I'm not sure how long you plan on staying in town, friend," he went on. "But perhaps you might want to think about making it a short stay."

"And why's that?" I said.

"It's a small town," he said. "Not enough room for everyone, if you get my meaning."

"I do," I said. "I get your meaning." I looked at my watch. "Oh my, I'm going to be late for work." I grabbed hold of my laptop, stuffed it under my arm.

"Work?" Big Billy said. "Thought you were just passing through."

"Need to make a few bucks first," I said. "Then I'll be on my way."

"And who would be stupid enough to hire you, little friend?" Big Billy asked.

"The owners of Loon Lake Inn," I said, staring directly into his eyes. "Maybe you've heard of them."

It wasn't like you could hear a pin drop at that point. It was like you could hear a feather falling to the floor. Turning, I went for the door. PJ stood in its way like a granite boulder.

"Let him through, PJ," Billy said. "Our little friend ain't seen the last of us."

"Thanks for the hospitality, Bunny," I said.

Opening the door, I let myself out, knowing full well that my boss, the owner and caretaker of Loon Lake Inn, was not only a member of the mob, but a high-ranking member bent on buying up Loon Lake. And doing so by force.

Vincent Zandri

12

As I crossed the parking lot on the way to my Jeep, I caught sight of a man who was staring at me from outside the front entrance of the sheriff's headquarters. Judging by the way he was dressed in a black-and-red-checked work shirt, blue jeans, cowboy boots, and a sidearm holstered to his belt, he had to be the sheriff himself. He nodded to me as I went around to the passenger side and set the laptop on the empty seat. Maybe he didn't say a word to me, but my gut sure did. It said, "Watch your back. Loon Lake isn't the lonely little paradise it seems to be."

The hand that came down on my shoulder felt like a sledge hammer. But I remained upright. Turning, I saw the massive bear of a man cock back his fist like he was John Wayne about to land a giant roundhouse. That was his first and last mistake. I landed two swift punches to his gut, then jabbed his neck directly on the Adam's apple. The pain and the lack of air was enough to drop him to his knees. He grabbed hold of his throat.

"Choking," he whispered painfully. "Choking."

"Sorry, Bill," I said. "But you should know better than to sneak up on a man like that."

For a quick second, I thought about stealing back my money. But then knowing he would only come calling on Bunny again, I decided against it.

"Be seeing you, Bill," I said.

"You're gonna regret the day we met, little friend," he said, his voice hoarse and broken. "I were you, I'd be leaving town immediately. Or else, you're a dead man."

"That hurts my feelings, Bill," I said.

I opened the Jeep door, slipped behind the wheel, and fired her up. Pulling out of the lot, I began to wonder what the hell I'd stepped into exactly. What kind of fate was at work when I'd decided to make the trip up to Loon Lake in the first place? Prison was beginning to seem like a safer place, the war in Iraq a safe haven, and my home with a wife and daughter who no longer cared for me, a happier situation.

I could have just kept on driving as I approached the turn that would take me back to Loon Lake Inn. I would find more money, and I could buy another typewriter somehow. But then as I slowed the Jeep and found myself turning onto the narrow gravel drive, my gut was telling me to stay. Not because I'd spent Sonny's money, but because I wanted his wife for my own. I wanted Cora to be my wife. I wanted to help her escape this place. I wanted to help her get out from under whatever the hell was going very wrong with this town. Maybe I wouldn't go so far as to help her kill her husband. But I would help her get the hell out. And that's all a man of limited means could hope to do.

I parked the Jeep, grabbed my laptop, and quickly made my way back to the secluded cabin. Inside, I plugged the laptop back in and washed myself up for work. Heading back over the trail to the tavern, I knew that I'd have to figure out a way to make change for the customers who would be bellying up to the bar in a matter of minutes. And do it quick. When I spotted the sheriff's prowler parked in the lot beside the Jeep, my stomach dropped to somewhere around my ankles. He wasn't here for a drink. Dollars to donuts, he was here to see me.

Once inside, I searched for Cora. She was behind the check-in counter looking so beautiful, I might have pulled her into the back room and made love to her on the spot. But I had to stay controlled and look like a professional.

"Where did you disappear to, Kingsley?" she asked, her face full of smiles.

She was back to being sweet, innocent Cora.

"Went into town for a few things," I lied.

For a split second, I thought about asking her for some money. But then I thought better of it. Maybe she and I had a thing going, but based on the New York Post account, it was her habit to have a thing going with somebody. Maybe a thing going with several men at once. Who knew what I was getting into by falling for her? All I knew was I wanted her so bad it hurt.

"Sonny's waiting for you, and he's not in the best of moods," she said.

"Something I said?" I offered, which seemed ridiculous considering I'd just had sex with his wife.

"It seems you're a sheriff magnet," she said.

"Sheriff's here to see me, Cora?"

She nodded, her smile no longer painting her face. "I'm on my way out to buy food for the kitchen," she said, grabbing hold of her car keys. "I'll check in on you later." She winked.

I turned for the tavern like a condemned man about to face the gallows.

Sonny was standing behind the bar. He was pouring a beer from the tap. When the mug was full, he placed it in front of the sheriff.

"On the house, Sheriff Woods," he said. Then, spotting me, "You're late, Kingsley. Hell of a way to start your first night."

He grinned almost maniacally when he said it. He wanted me to think he was joking, but I sensed some seriousness in his delivery. Some real anger. Maybe he was testing me to see if I would walk the hell out. But then, I suspected he must have known his wife was the one thing that would keep me around. How the hell could he not have heard us having sex from outside the cabin beyond the trees? How could he not have heard his wife's passionate screams? Fact is, he must have heard us. And now that he knew how much I liked his wife…how much I lusted for her…he knew he had power over me. Because no way I was leaving this place without her.

Sonny excused himself to the sheriff and made his way back into the kitchen. That left me alone with the upstate lawman. I tried to familiarize myself with the bar back while he quietly sipped his beer. The atmosphere was tense because we both knew why he was here. When I had no choice but to turn around and face him, I pursed my lips and nodded.

He drank some beer, wiped the foam from his mouth with the back of his hand.

"You are indeed late, Mr. Kingsley," he said. "And the Albany County Parole Board knows it."

"Pardon me?" I said.

He was wearing that same red-and-black-checked shirt and jeans that he was wearing when I saw him standing outside his office. He was also wearing his cowboy hat, and his long, narrow face was covered in salt and pepper scruff. His eyes were blue and his body was long and hard like a jogger or maybe even a marathoner. Even though I couldn't see his weapon, I knew he had to be packing the semi-automatic I'd noticed earlier.

He said, "You should have called your parole officer by three o'clock this afternoon for your first check-in. You got a sweet deal not having to report to a halfway house. Be a shame to jeopardize that situation."

He drank more beer. I had to admit, with everything that had happened since I walked out the gates of Sing Sing, I'd totally forgot to call my parole officer. I'd have to make the call sooner than later.

"You know who I am," I said like a question. "How'd you manage that?"

He stretched his hands over the bar.

"Where are my manners?" he said. "I'm Sheriff Kevin Woods. You're Mr. Jonathan or JA Kingsley. But everyone just calls you Kingsley."

I felt a tightness in my stomach.

"How'd you guess that, Sheriff?" I said.

He glanced at the kitchen door as if he suspected Sonny had his ear pressed against it on the other side.

"Part of my job is to run license plates when sufficiently warranted."

I pictured my Jeep. The license plate attached to the back bumper. I couldn't even begin to recite the letters and numbers on it. I was just happy to have it back after being without it for all that time. For all I knew, Leslie might have sold it out from under me. Not because she needed the money. Her family had more than enough money, and they were always willing to hand over as much as she demanded when she demanded it. Maybe therein lay the overall problem. Leslie, and Erin for that matter, never really needed me. And when I went to the joint, they had no use for me. But I'm getting off topic.

"And you decided to run mine," I said.

His ten spot was laid out on the bar. I was holding off on making change for him simply because I didn't have any change to give him.

"Never seen your Jeep before. This is a sleepy town.

Even in high season, folks rather head over to Lake George or Lake Placid. Good Christ, we can't even begin to compete with Lake Placid. Even little Paradox Lake does better than us." He pursed his lips, shrugged his shoulders like he felt defeated. "We're just a lonely little lakeside community that time forgot."

In my head, I pictured Big Billy demanding an illegal payout from Bunny.

"Maybe a big investor will come along and drop a whole lot of cash on a Sandals Resort or something like that," I said.

It was a jest and seemed to make his sad face brighten up a little.

"Funny you should say that, Mr. Kingsley," he said.

I told him to call me Kingsley.

"Well, Kingsley," he said, "seems Loon Lake does indeed have an interested investor. Problem is, said investor is not exactly the kind of money we're looking for."

I shook my head like I didn't understand. But I was beginning to get it alright. Those goons who roughed up Bunny for their monthly blood money. They worked for my new boss.

"Tell you what," I said, turning, grabbing the bottle of Jameson off the top shelf, "I'll join you for one, Sheriff Woods."

I poured a shot, held it up as if to say cheers, and downed it in one swift pull. I preferred to sip my whiskey, but I didn't want to risk Torchi seeing me drink from Loon Lake Inn's stash, so I downed it quickly.

I leaned closer to the lawman.

"Torchi," I said.

He looked over one shoulder and then the other.

"Here's the deal, Kingsley," he said. "He's not top tier in the Queens-based syndicate, but he's worked his way up far from the bottom, and he did it by becoming one of the best ambulance chasing lawyers and fixers in Manhattan.

He's still under the misguided impression that no one in this town knows who the hell he really is, nor the dangers he poses."

I shook my head. "I don't get it. Why would an active mob member become a lawyer?"

"Not only gives him an air of legitimacy and respect, but he's forced to deal with the law and the DA on a daily basis. I'm sure that's the way the family had it planned for him all along."

"I get it," I said, pouring a second shot. "It's like that ancient book, The Art of War. Keep your friends close, but your enemies closer."

"You should know that being a professional solider and an ex-con, Kingsley," he said.

He finished his beer, and I poured him another. Again, I let his ten spot lie there on the bar only a half inch away from a condensate ring.

"So, where's this going?" I said. "Why do I get the feeling you want something from me, and it has nothing to do with my parole officer?"

He sipped some of the fresh beer.

"I saw the way you handled that biker crew. They think they own the town now that Torchi has put bids in on every business and residence not only on Main Street but the entire lake—the portion that doesn't qualify as state land anyway."

"How much he willing to spend?"

"Tens of millions."

"So, why don't people take the cash and get the hell out?"

"People here are simple, Kingsley," he explained. "They spent their whole life here, and so did their parents, and their parents."

"Money talks, Sheriff."

"Yes, it does," he said. "But those millions Torchi and his bosses are willing to part with ain't going into the buyouts. They're going into the lake's redevelopment."

I nodded. "He's paying pennies."

"That he is," the sheriff said. "A couple of people have sold out, but many more haven't and won't, no matter the offer. The businesses like Bunny's, who refuse to sell, are being choked out. Torchi makes them pay him a monthly rent like he already owns the properties. And they don't dare sell to someone with a higher bid for fear of their lives."

"That's extortion," I said. "Why don't you arrest him?"

He ran his hand down over his tight face. "He's threatened retribution should I get tough on him with the law. There's more, but I can't get into it right now."

"Give me a hint."

He leaned in closer so that he could speak under his breath.

"You might have noticed that burned out house in the middle of town."

"The one with the crime scene ribbon wrapped around the front door?"

"That's Torchi's work. An entire family died in that fire."

"No arrest?"

"The state police are on the take, Kingsley. On his payroll."

I poured another shot, drank that down.

"Jesus Christ, you have a big problem, Sheriff," I said.

"I just can't risk arresting Sonny," he added. Then he looked down into his beer, like he was reliving a whole bunch of bad memories.

I said, "Okay, so Torchi, my present boss, is terrorizing the town with his three goons. He's already killed an entire family, and the state police are on the take. You're powerless, and the community doesn't know where to turn. What the hell you want me to do about it?"

"You're working at Torchi's inn. Means you're already on the inside. You can observe things for me. Keep me informed."

If only he knew I'd just had wild sex with the boss's wife.

"Also, this town could use a little muscle. Someone to stand up to Billy and his merry band of thugs. You're the kind who can take care of business. Looks to me like you learned a thing or two on the battlefield and while you were in the joint."

"I survived, but I ain't exactly Rambo," I said. "But listen, Sheriff, I'm not so sure Torchi will take to my beating his men at will. Maybe it's you who needs to stiffen up his backbone."

He gazed into my eyes then. His eyes were colder and harder than granite. The stare spoke to me. It told me he was tough, but that he just couldn't risk the lives of his residents.

"Torchi is playing totally dumb," he went on. "Thus the smiley face while he poured me a free beer. He pretends he has no idea who those three bikers are. He's still playing the country gentleman caretaker ruse. But I know he wants to take over this town and then use it to sell his family's personally manufactured drugs."

"His wife, Cora," I said.

"What about her?"

His face grew tight. Like I'd hit a nerve.

"He loves her," the sheriff went on. "Maybe by now you've gathered how she feels about him."

"Apparently, she's just one more Loon Lake resident who's become his slave."

He drank down the rest of his beer and slid off his stool. "If you help me," he said, "I'll make it worth your while."

"Yes, you will," I said. "But what happens if I decide not to get involved?"

"They'll come after us," he said. "The Queens contingent, I mean. And it won't be just three bikers with beer bellies this time."

"Still say you should call in the police. The state troopers can't all be on the take."

He shook his head like he meant it.

"Can't take that chance. They'll burn the whole town with every man, woman, and child in it."

"So, you want my help...need my help. But I'm just one man, Sheriff."

"You're the first civilian around here to stand up to those bastards."

"That Big Billy pissed me off. Plus, he tried to hurt my feelings."

"Something tells me you live your life like you got nothing to lose, Kingsley. Loon Lake is at war whether it knows it or not."

"You want me to drive them out on my own."

"I want you to put the fear in them that I can't. And you have my blessing to do whatever it takes. You will not be arrested. You got that? If you cut their heads off and stick them on stakes, you will not face charges, at least not from my office. That, I can guarantee you."

I poured and downed one last shot.

"Could get ugly, Sheriff. Especially if what you say is true and they come after us with everything they got."

"We'll be ready for them if they do. Just tell me what you need to make it happen. I'll give you everything in my power."

"Everything?"

"Everything and anything."

I thought about it for a minute. I desperately needed money. I was also falling in love with Cora. Lastly, I needed a story. Something that would make a great book.

"What can you afford?" I asked.

"One-hundred-thousand. It's my personal pension."

"And Cora," I said. "Cora remains innocent. No matter what."

"Like I said, watch your back when it comes to the caretaker's wife. Sonny wants nothing more than to take over this town, but if he catches you with her, he'll kill you, and he'll make it painful and slow. Death by a thousand cuts."

I nodded and felt a chill run up and down my backbone.

Sonny had already caught us cheating. So, why, then, was he letting me live?

"You can start by giving me two-hundred dollars, Sheriff," I said.

He smiled wryly, dug into his pocket, pulled out his bankroll. He counted it.

"One-hundred-twenty-three and some change do?"

"It'll have to."

He handed me the cash. I brought it to the cash register, opened the drawer, and tossed it inside. Just then, a commotion, and the kitchen door opened.

Sonny stepped back into the bar.

13

"Sheriff Woods," Sonny barked. "You're still here." He was wearing that stained apron again. He was wiping his hands with it. His brow was beaded with sweat, his gray/black hair slicked back against his skull, his face bearing the usual scruff, and his belly filled out the apron like he was pregnant with a basketball. He stepped into the bar back.

"Kingsley, my good man," he said. "The sheriff drinks for free."

"You don't have to do that, Mr. Torchi," Woods said.

"Nonsense," Sonny said. "You're the sheriff. We all depend on you for our safety and security in this town. Isn't that right, Kingsley?"

I nodded.

"Oh," Sonny went on. "I assume you and the sheriff are well acquainted by now, Kingsley."

"We've been chatting it up," Woods added.

"Then you know what a well-respected novelist Kingsley is. He's here working on a new book." He smacked me on the back so hard I thought my lungs might bust through my ribs. "He's a little short on cash right now, so in exchange for a cabin rental he's gonna become the caretaker's apprentice. Isn't that right, Kingsley?"

I cleared my throat of something bitter and foul tasting. Tried to smile.

"You betcha, boss," I said.

He pulled Sheriff Woods's empty mug off the bar, filled it with beer from the tap.

"Kingsley also gets along swimmingly with Cora," Sonny went on. "Glad somebody does." He slapped my back again. "That's a joke. Get it?"

Nobody laughed.

"Well then," Torchi went on, "I'll be headed back into the kitchen to finish dinner. Expecting some patrons later on. Money don't grow on trees, and I gotta make it while I can."

He left the bar back for the swinging kitchen door. But just before he got to it, he turned back around.

"Oh, Sheriff," he said. "While I got you here, I was wondering…you hearing any scuttlebutt from the residents about selling out to a developer?"

I felt a little start in my heart. I was sure the sheriff did too.

"Why do you ask, Sonny?" he asked.

"Oh, I'm just wondering who's doing the buying and if people are willing to sell. Be a shame for the fine folks of this sleepy little town to let an opportunity to make some real money go to waste. Imagine Loon Lake becoming a real tourist destination like Lake Placid or Lake George? Now, that would really be something, wouldn't it, Sheriff? It would mean a major raise for you. Maybe a new station and, hell, a nice new house."

"I suppose it would, Sonny," he said.

"Be seeing you around, Sheriff," Sonny said.

"Be seeing you too," Woods said. "Thanks for the

beers."

Sonny disappeared behind the door. The sheriff looked me in the eye.

"Think about my offer," he said. "One-hundred K. The law need not apply."

"I will," I said. "Maybe we should just start at the top and get rid of the boss."

"You mean like cut off the head of the snake?"

"Something like that."

"So long as the snake doesn't grow three or four more heads and starts biting the hell out of this town out of revenge. The snake is long, and its tail resides in Queens, New York."

As he turned to leave, I already knew I was going to help the sheriff rid Loon Lake of Sonny Torchi, snake that he was. Not because I wanted to help Loon Lake or even grab myself an easy one-hundred-thousand dollars. But only because I wanted Cora all to myself.

I found a pack of smokes behind the bar near the sink. Since no one occupied the tavern other than me, my guess is they belonged to Sonny. The vape device he occasionally sucked on was his way of trying to kick the habit. I decided to head out onto the front porch and light up. I never smoked much in the joint since it was strictly forbidden. But every now and again a CO—one of the good ones—who took a liking to you might pull you aside, allow you to join them outside in the corrections officers' smoking area. It was a little glass-enclosed place they referred to as The Lounge. They'd ask you your life story, and if you were like me and didn't outwardly appear like the violent criminal type—a swastika tattoo didn't cover my face, for instance—they would inevitably ask, "How the hell did a dude like you end up in a joint like this?" And you know what I'd tell them? "Why don't you ask my wife?"

Usually, they'd nod sadly, and without saying another word, they knew precisely where I was coming from. Because maybe screws could head home at night after a long day locked up inside the iron house. But that didn't mean they weren't any less a prisoner than I was. As soon as they walked through the door at night and closed it behind them, they, too, were subject to a different kind of incarceration. "How the hell did a dude like you end up in a place like this?" they'd ask themselves while looking in the mirror.

The smoke I was inhaling now...the bitter taste of burning tobacco, the nicotine rush inside my blood, the cotton mouth...it brought me back to Sing Sing, and the sad faces of all those screws. My heart went out to them almost as much as it did the pathetic lifers who would never see the light of a free day again. They were alive in the physical sense, but for all intents and purposes, they were so very dead. Dead men walking. Zombies, all of them.

The truck pulled up and parked beside my Jeep. It was Cora. She got out, looking beautiful in her tight jeans, cowboy boots, and work shirt unbuttoned enough that I could see her hard breasts under that black pushup bra. My sex got immediately hard, and I knew I had to take her again before I headed back in the tavern. When she grabbed a couple sacks of groceries, I stepped down off the porch, dropped the cigarette to the gravel and stamped it out. Then I went to her.

"Here," I said, "let me help."

When I took the bags from her, my hands brushed against hers. It made my stomach tight and my throat close in on itself. My body was shaking. What the hell was happening to me? Were my feelings for Cora because I hadn't had a woman in so much time that it hurt? Was it because Leslie left me and took our daughter with her?

Then there was the sheriff. His offer of helping me destroy Torchi and his plan to take over Loon Lake and do it by force if necessary. Maybe I was still in prison, and this whole thing was an elaborate dream. Maybe I'd finally lost it, and right now, I was strapped to a bed inside a psych ward. But then, what the hell difference did it make? This was my reality whether I liked it or not.

"I want you now," I said to her face. "I want you again." She focused not on me but on the tavern door. Like any minute her husband might walk out of it. I couldn't blame her one bit. But I didn't give a fuck about her husband. I only knew what I wanted right now. I grabbed her by the arm, yanked her to me, and kissed her hard on the mouth. She punched my chest, clawed herself off of me.

"Are you crazy?"

I smiled. "Yeah," I said. "Out of my mind."

I felt a small trickle of blood oozing from my sternum, down over my belly. Cora had cut me with her fingernails. The pain felt good. It made me happy. It made me want her all the more.

"If my husband sees you, he'll kill you," she said. "Don't you get it?"

"Don't fool yourself, Cora. He already has."

"You don't know that, Kingsley."

"He heard us fucking inside the cabin, and you know it. I thought you wanted him dead."

"I do," she said. "But not like this."

I recalled my plan.

"Tomorrow," I said. "Tomorrow while I'm clearing the trails with him...there'll be an accident."

She looked at me with a stone face. It was unlike any expression I'd seen her use before.

"It's all happening so quick," she said. "I don't even know you."

"A person knows when they love someone. They know right away. Do you love me, Cora?"

She looked at me while I held the plastic grocery bags in both my hands.

"Yes," she said. "I love you, Kingsley."

"Do you trust me?"

"I trust you."

"Tomorrow," I said. "Tomorrow, I take care of our little

problem. I'll also be one-hundred-thousand dollars richer."

Her brown eyes suddenly widened.

"How—"

"Don't ask questions I can't answer right now. Do you hear what I'm saying, Cora?"

Then came the roar of motorcycles approaching over the long gravel drive. Without seeing who was driving them, I knew who they were. Big Billy and his crew of goons. Setting the bags to the ground, I pulled Cora into me, kissed her so hard I thought her lip might start bleeding again.

"Come see me tonight," I said. "It might be the last time we can be together for a long time if my plan for tomorrow works."

"Why do you say that?"

"Because if I kill your husband, we can't chance being seen together for a while. You will have to go into a serious period of mourning. You'll really have to pour it on."

The motorcycles were getting louder. When the bikers pulled into the parking lot, I knew my gut instincts were right on. Big Billy looked right at me.

"I'd better get back inside," I said. "Those meatheads are going to be thirsty."

Releasing Cora from my hold, I picked the bags back up and started for the tavern porch.

"I'll bring these to the kitchen. See you tonight, baby."

"I'll be there," she said.

As I was making the steps up onto the porch, I heard Big Billy bark, "Well hello beautiful Cora, baby."

I knew then, in my heart of hearts, that I would find a way for the big biker bastard to suffer a terrible accident, too.

14

I went straight to the kitchen, where Sonny was stirring something in a pot. It smelled like spaghetti sauce. Setting the bags on the butcher block counter, I turned to leave. But he called out to me.

"What is it, boss?" I said, stealing a closer look at the piping hot, bubbling sauce.

"Tell me what you think, Kingsley," he said, holding a ladle in one hand and cupping his other hand under it to catch whatever spillage might occur.

The truth? I wanted nothing more than the grab hold of his neck and stick his head into the boiling cauldron of red sauce. I'd hold him down until his lungs filled and he drowned in the shit. But that was no way to kill a man like Torchi. It would be way too obvious, and not even a vengeful lawman like Woods would be able to save my sorry ass from an arrest at that point.

Dutifully, I stepped up to the spoon and tasted the hot sauce. Here's the thing. It might have been really hot, but I'll be damned if that wasn't some of the best spaghetti sauce I ever tasted. Or maybe by then, I was so used to prison food that dog shit would have tasted good. He seemed pleased that I loved his recipe. Every meal I'd had at Loon Lake Inn thus far was off the charts good. Hell, maybe Sonny was poisoning me. I wiped my mouth with the back of my hand, smiled.

"That's good shit, boss," I said.

He slapped me on the back again. It made me want to kill him even more.

"Love it when you call me, boss," he said. "I don't even get that kind of respect from my employees." Then, realizing what he just said. "Not that I have any employees. But if I did…" He allowed the gaff to trail off like a bad fart.

"Got some dudes in the bar," I said, knowing they were the very employees he was letting on about. "Thirsty dudes by the looks of them."

He went back to stirring his sauce.

"Let me know if they give you any trouble, Kingsley," he said.

"I can handle myself," I said.

His grin reminded me of a clown. A bad clown.

"Bet you can," he said. "That's why I like you."

I escaped the kitchen.

Big Billy locked eyes on me as soon as I made it through the door. I was ready for him to jump me, but it never happened. Instead, all three of them pretended they'd never seen me before. They acted like I was never present inside Bunny's bar, never gave her the cash to pay her monthly blood money, never dropped Billy in the parking lot. They mumbled shit among themselves and then ordered a round of draft beers and whiskey chasers. I didn't bother to ask them to pay.

They drank in silence while I stood with my back pressed against the bar.

Billy drank his shot and followed up with a drink of his beer that emptied half the glass. The others did the same. I got the feeling if Billy decided to sip his drinks, they would have done that also. Their every move depended on his. When he drank down the rest of the beer, he slid off his stool. The other two slid off their stools and made for the door. They didn't leave but instead, stood guard over the exit.

Billy pointed at me, then made a curling gesture with his index finger that told me he wanted me to come closer. Why give the big guy a problem when I had already embarrassed him in front of his crew?

"Another drink, Bill?" I said.

He leaned in to me, his lips so close to my ear I could feel his hot halitosis.

"Remember what I said about you leaving town, son," he said. "You got lucky with me once. Trust me when I tell you it won't happen again. Do we have an understanding?"

"By all means," I said, pursing my lips.

"Good," he said. "Now, I have to get back to work." He turned and made his way into the kitchen.

No trout fishermen showed up that night, so Sonny decided to let me close up early.

"Some friends in for dinner," he said. "Just the guys." Naturally, I knew who his friends were…his employees.

I also knew what they'd be discussing over his spaghetti and meatball dinner. They'd be talking about Loon Lake, their plan to take it over for the real bosses down in Queens. They would also be discussing me. Would Big Billy admit to my putting him down outside Bunny's Place? Maybe. Would Sonny tell them he suspected me of fucking his wife? Maybe. Was I walking into a hornet's nest over my lust and love for a woman I barely even knew? Most definitely.

I managed to steal a drink of Jameson from out of the bottle without Sonny seeing me before I came around the bar and started for the door. Going with my gut, I sensed he wouldn't bother with counting the till, so I also quietly opened the drawer, slipped out a twenty and stuffed it into my pocket. He was seated at one of the big round tables in the dining room near the stone fireplace, along with the three black leather-clad bikers. Only Big Billy was eyeballing me when I shot them a quick glance. Slowly, he ran his index finger across his neck. He then stuck his tongue out and flicked it at me like a snake.

I might have succeeded at proving how tough I was, but for some reason, that little throat cutting gesture chilled me to the bone. I left the tavern without saying goodnight to my new boss.

Crossing over the narrow trail in the dark, I made a mental note of buying a flashlight. Or maybe there would already be one inside my cabin. I needed something more to drink than just that shot of Jameson I'd stolen. There was more beer in the refrigerator. I would rather have whiskey, but beer would have to do for now.

Stepping up onto the small porch, I opened the cabin door and saw that a candle was burning. When I looked at the bed over my shoulder, I saw that Cora was already waiting for me. I felt my pulse elevate and my breathing grow shallow. She was sitting up in bed, her breasts bare as the day she was born and pointing at me. She was sipping red wine from a long-stemmed glass.

"I thought you'd never make it home," she said, her eyes radiant in the glow of the candlelight.

"Home," I said. "What's that?"

She sipped her wine.

"Don't you have a home, Kingsley?" she asked. "Everybody's got to have a home."

She'd already set out a glass for me on the table beside the uncorked bottle of red. I picked the bottle up, poured myself a glass. I couldn't remember the last time I shared a good wine with a pretty woman…a gorgeous woman. Leslie

134

didn't drink. Not even the occasional glass of wine. But now, I was enjoying a fine wine with an even finer woman. A woman who was both beautiful and naked.

"I might remind you that your husband is currently only about one-hundred yards away having dinner with his employees."

"First of all," she said, "they will be there for hours, especially once they dig into the tavern's booze."

"Second of all?" I asked, sitting on the end of the bed.

"Second of all," she said, "how did you know those men work for my husband?"

"I ran into them in town earlier. Big Billy shook down the owner of Bunny's bar. I know what Sonny's up to. Or should I say, I know what his mob bosses are up to down in Queens. They want to take over Loon Lake, turn it into a tourist destination. They want to force the residents out and fill it with drug hungry tourists. They'll get violent if they have to, and the sheriff says he's powerless over it all. He said that Sonny burned a family who wouldn't cooperate and that the state police are on the take."

She just looked at me like I was reciting some dangerous shit. I was.

"Looks like you're finally getting some of your questions answered, Kingsley," she said.

"How did you ever get mixed up with a guy like Sonny, Cora?" I begged.

Of course, I already knew how she'd originally gotten involved with him. But I wanted her version of the story. She sipped some wine for courage, then exhaled.

"I got into some trouble," she said, looking not at me but down into her wine where the memory must have been replaying itself. "Would you believe I used to be a New York City cop?"

Of course, I knew it, but I didn't want to let on that I knew it.

She said, "I got into it with some new recruits. We did

135

a little good-natured partying but eventually took a wrong turn on a bad stretch of road, so to speak."

"You're losing me," I lied.

She lifted her head, brushed her thick hair back with her free hand, and looked me in the eyes.

"We all started having sex together, Kingsley. You know...S. E. X."

"Sex," I said, like a question.

"We'd drop some Molly, get all liquored up, and pretty much go to bed." She drank a little more wine. "I know it sounds seedy, but we were all adults, and it was all consensual, and even well-intentioned if you can believe it." There was hesitation in her voice.

"I'm sensing a but here," I said.

"Something happened that I didn't count on."

I stole my first sip of the wine. It was good. More than pretty good. Dry, crisp, filled with flavor. Not like the cheap wine and ripple some of the dirt poor inmates used to dream about in their sleep.

"One of the participating cops secretly videoed one of our sessions. He presented it to the IG, and just like that, I was busted. He even got me on film dropping the Molly."

She made the same throat cutting gesture that Big Billy had made earlier. "Just like that, career over. And I mean, career...fucking...over."

"They take away your pension?" Again, I already knew the answer to the question, but it felt natural asking it anyway.

"That was just the start of it. They wanted to arrest me for possession of stolen evidence."

"The Molly?"

"Yup. That alone would have put me behind bars for a year or more. And you know what happens to cops behind bars."

That might have been the segue into telling her about my little vacation in the iron house. But I decided to let it slide. Besides, just like her, my past wasn't exactly hidden from public view. I wasn't the most popular author in the world, not by a long shot. You wouldn't find my mystery novels placed on the table at the front of Barnes and Nobles along with the Pattersons and Baldaccis. But you could find all my books online, and I still had an audience significant enough that when I was sent down to Sing Sing, I made not only the local news but national news too.

"Not a good situation," I said weakly.

"So, I lawyered up."

"Sonny," I said.

"He was a powerhouse lawyer, and it was no secret who his family was. I knew it would cost me, but no way in hell was I about to let the cop hating Southern District prosecutors make an example out of me. So, I threw it all into Sonny's lap, and he destroyed them."

"What do you mean by destroyed?"

"He not only got them to drop the charges about the stolen evidence, he saved my pension. He wasn't able to save my job, but by then, the very idea of staying a cop made me nauseous."

"And for his services? How much did he charge?"

She drank down her glass of wine, then slipped out of bed, her perfect naked ass staring back at me like heaven itself.

"He made me have sex with him, of course," she said while pouring herself more wine. "I saw that one coming from a mile away. But what I didn't see coming was his proposal of marriage."

"He forced you into marrying him?"

She turned, and I looked at her trimmed pussy, and I wanted it more than I wanted anything else in the world. But not yet. First, I wanted more from her. I wanted her full story.

"If I didn't marry him, he said he would make sure his case to save my ass failed. He's a Torchi. He could make the DA shine his shoes if he wanted."

"So, you married him."

She nodded and went back to staring into her wine. "I married him, and we bought this place and left New York City for good."

"But now he has big plans."

"He always has big plans, Kingsley. His family and their syndicate have big plans, and they always revolve around selling heroin to innocent suburban kids."

"The sheriff wants him stopped, and he's offered to pay me to help him."

"I guess that makes two of us."

"You and the sheriff have something very unique in common. You want to see Sonny Torchi dead."

She exhaled again.

"It sounds horrible when you put it that way."

"But it's the truth, Cora."

"You're right, Kingsley."

"Tomorrow, I'll make it happen," I said. "And then, we don't see one another for a while. Sheriff Woods is gonna protect me, but that won't stop the staties—the clean ones, anyway—from sticking their nose in it."

"I get it," she said. "And I love you for it, Kingsley." She set her wine on the nightstand. Without a word, she shifted herself so that her face was hovering over my cock. She pulled me out and took me in her mouth and started working me slowly and sweetly. She knew how to use her hand, her mouth, and her tongue all at the same time. She was a pro, and she knew it. I was so hard and so filled up with juice that she didn't have to work for very long before I told her I was about to come. I expected her to free her mouth of my cock but instead, she just worked all the harder. When I came, she swallowed every bit of it, not like she wanted nothing more than to please me, but like she lived on the stuff the same way a junkie lived for the chemical high. It was the best head I'd ever received, hands down.

But we didn't stop there. I turned her over onto her back, kissed her titties and suckled her nipples until she couldn't take it anymore. Couldn't take the sweet, biting pain. Then I ran my tongue and lips down her flat belly until I came to her pussy. I worked on her clit like I wanted to push myself all the way inside her body...like I wanted to crawl up into her heart and curl my body around the beating, pulsing organ.

When she came, she thrust her hips so violently she scared the living daylights out of me. She was a wild, untamed beast. Orgasms were her drug of choice. I knew just one wouldn't be enough because she grabbed the back of my head with both hands and made me work on her some more until she came again, this time came like a gusher, and I nearly drowned in her waterfall of wetness. It was something to behold, and it all made me so hard again that I immediately mounted her. I didn't make love to her. She was beyond something as tame as that. She wanted to get fucked, and she wanted to get fucked as hard as I could thrust my hard, pulsating eight inches into her. She wanted me to stab her with it. She wanted me to make it hurt. She wanted me to impale her. And when I couldn't hold it in anymore, I pulled it out and exploded all over her bare breasts. Her smile told me she loved every bit of it.

For a short time, she rested her head on my chest and ran her fingertips over the many scars that mapped it, including the new wound she personally delivered outside in the parking lot earlier. But then, almost abruptly, she got up from the bed, made her way into the little bathroom. I heard the water going and then the toilet flush.

When she came back in, she started getting dressed. As she put on her black thong panties, I started getting excited again. It had been so long for me, I was convinced I could give it to her again. But I knew she was having no part of it. Not any longer. This was the second time I'd fucked Cora in a single day, and I already knew what kind of woman she was. She was the type who made a sea change after sex. Especially rough sex. Some women wanted to cuddle. Others cried, the tears streaming down their cheeks. Still, others turned stone cold, as if they were pissed off at you for making them undergo multiple orgasms…like it was an insult to their physical and emotional being.

The last one was the category Cora fell under, and even though I knew it wasn't the best omen for our relationship, I was still crazy about her, which meant I would just have to find a way to deal with it.

When she was fully dressed, she made her way to the door. As she put her hands on the knob, she looked at me over her shoulder.

"Tomorrow," she said. "Tomorrow, it happens."

"Yes," I said. And then I added, "God willing." Why I felt the need to invoke God in the homicidal proceedings was beyond me, but I did it anyway. Maybe it was the devil doing the talking. A lot of people wanted Torchi dead. But apparently, God and I were the only ones willing to do the dirty work.

Her laser-like eyes were still cutting into me.

"Prison," she said, "was it hard?"

So, she knew about my past after all. I guess it wasn't all that difficult to figure out. The internet made everything public.

"Harder than the war even," I said.

"The scars on your chest and back," she said. "They're bad."

"Yeah," I said. "But I survived."

"But my husband will not." She exhaled. "Sorry about scratching you earlier."

"I liked it," I said.

"Where the hell did you come from?" she said.

"You just answered your own question," I said.

Cora opened the door then and left the cabin without saying goodbye.

15

In the dream, we're standing at the altar. Leslie and I. It's a bit strange because Erin is there too, standing right beside the priest, even though she's years away from being born. My daughter is wearing jeans and a black t-shirt that says The Doors. Her shoulder-length black hair is dyed blonde. The priest is bald and fat and dressed in a white robe. He's speaking to us, but his voice sounds tinny and strange. Like a mechanical voice. He's not breathing through his mouth but instead, through a hole in his neck. He's a neck breather. He's got a trach in his neck and every time he takes a breath it sounds like he's choking on his own air.

"Do you take this woman to be your lawfully wedded wife?" he asks in his robot voice.

I gaze at Leslie. She's lovely in her long black hair, black gown, black eyes, and black heart.

"I do," I say.

"Thank God," Erin says, "or else I won't be born."

The priest shifts his focus to Leslie.

"Do you take this man to be your lawfully wedded husband?" he asks. "Do you promise to fuck him over, to cheat on him, to suck up every penny he makes, and then abandon him when he goes to prison for kicking the shit out of the dickless prick you were boning behind his back?"

"I do," she says.

"Don't do it, mom," Erin says. "But then what am I saying? You have to say yes or I won't be born."

The priest is now bleeding through the hole in his throat. The blood is bubbling, and the sound of gurgling is making me sick to my stomach. Soon, the bleeding isn't only coming from his throat but also from his mouth and nostrils. Erin steals a wide-eyed look at him and takes a couple of steps backward.

"Gag me, why don't you," she says. "See what you did now, Dad?"

I want to tell her it's not my fault, but it's impossible for me to speak. It's almost like I don't have a mouth.

Leslie stares me down with I-hate-your-guts eyes.

"You're a real asshole, Kingsley," she says. "I want a divorce."

A man steps up onto the altar. He's the big carpenter. His face is all cut up from my tossing him through the plate glass window. His head is bleeding, and a portion of his pink brain is exposed. He proceeds to make out with Leslie right on the altar. They're really going at it with their pink tongues. I look past the priest to Christ hanging from the wooden cross.

"Can you believe this shit, Lord?" I pose. "The nerve of these two."

"Humans are truly screwed up," he says. "You're all better off just killing yourselves sooner than later."

Someone's knocking on the door. Correction. Not knocking, but pounding. I sat up straight, gazed at my watch. Five in the morning. Jesus H, when did I fall to sleep? I fumbled for the bedside lamp, turned it on.

The Caretaker's Wife

"Just a minute!" I barked.

"Come on, Kingsley," came the voice through the wood door. "Time to rise and shine. We got work to do today."

He was trying to open the door, but I must have locked it after Cora left last night. There's an empty wine bottle set on the nightstand and five beer cans. I had way too much to drink and passed out. It's not the first time I'd drank too much since coming to this lake, but it's the first time I'd been on a mini-bender in a long, long time and my body wasn't used to that much alcohol all at once. I knew I'd better taper it off or my liver was going to explode.

Slipping out of bed, I felt the pounding in my head and the cotton in my mouth and all I wanted to do was go back to bed. But I had a job to do today. No, scratch that, I had more than a job to do today, and the sooner I got it done, the better. I went to the door, fumbled with the deadbolt until it released, and opened the door.

Sonny was standing there dressed in a long-sleeve khaki shirt, his belly protruding against it. He was wearing an old New York Yankees baseball cap on his head, and, as usual, his face was scruffy. I could smell his sour breath, which didn't do a hell of a lot for my weak stomach. I looked for any sign that he might be packing his semi-automatic. I didn't see any. But that didn't mean he wasn't carrying it. For all I knew, it was strapped to his ankle. For all I knew, he was going to get me all the way out in the woods and shoot me in the head as payback for messing with his wife.

"Tie one on last night, buddy?" he said. "What's with writers and drinking? You all think you're Hemingway or something." He barged his way inside. "Come on, put some pants on. We got trails to clear. This place ain't no freebie. Chop, chop."

Here's what I was thinking: Maybe I should just kill the son of a bitch right now. Maybe I should slip into the kitchen, grab a steak knife, and jab it into his throat a hundred times and allow him to bleed out all over the floor. I could go back to bed, and only when I was ready to wake up, would I wrap his body up with rope and cement blocks and toss him in the lake.

But if that wasn't a stupid-ass idea, then I didn't know what the hell was. I pulled my jeans off the bed, slipped into them while he watched. I then slipped on my boots and threw on my work shirt.

"Mind if I wash my face and make a cup of coffee?" I said.

"Go ahead and wash up," he said. "Coffee can wait till we take a break."

"I can hardly wait, boss," I said, my voice filled with acid.

I went to the kitchen sink, turned on the cold water. While I put my head under the steady stream of freezing cold water, I could hear him walking around the place.

"You wanna know something, Kingsley?" he said. "If I didn't know any better, I'd say this place smells like pussy."

His comment sent a shock up and down my backbone. It was almost better than downing a cup of black coffee—in terms of sobering me up, that is. I allowed the cold water to drown me while he went on pacing.

"And you know what, Kingsley? The pussy…the fragrance…it smells real familiar. Shit, if I didn't know any better, I'd say you're fucking my wife."

That did it. It woke me right up. I didn't even need coffee by that point. Pulling my head out from under the water, I dried myself with the dishrag that hung over the spigot.

"If you're smelling pussy, boss," I said, "it must be coming from you, because the only action this place has seen is me and Rosy Palm."

He pointed at me with an extended index finger. "Now that's an image I can do without, Kingsley," he said. Then, looking at his watch, "You ready? It will be daylight in a few minutes, and I want to already be on the trail."

"Yeah," I said, "I'm ready."

He went for the door.

"Oh, and one more thing," he went on. "Unless you've already taken your morning constitutional, I'd strongly suggest you take a toilet paper roll. You never know when last night's meal is gonna wanna escape."

"I'll be fine," I said.

"Suit yourself. I gotta warn you, however, shitting in the woods can be real uncomfortable without some TP."

But by then, shitting in the forest was the last thing on my mind.

We hiked the narrow path, then made our way across the lawn past the main cabins until we came to the back of the tavern where Sonny had already set out an older model chainsaw along with a plastic jug of gasoline and another one that was filled with motor oil.

"I'll run the chainsaw," he said, nodding at the stuff, "and you carry the gas and oil. You'll also clear away the branches and twigs as I cut them. Be prepared to sweat that booze out of your system, Kingsley. Hope you can handle it."

I grabbed the two cans by their handles, felt their weight, and the toxic liquid sloshing around inside them.

"Don't worry about me, boss," I said.

He smiled. "Who said I was worried, Kingsley?"

I still didn't have a clue how I was going to make Sonny's accident happen. Only that I wanted to make it happen. Anything could happen in the deep woods. A man could trip on a root, and he might fall face first onto a rock. Or maybe he could get torn apart by a wild animal. Like Sonny told me at breakfast yesterday, there was an angry black bear roaming the woods. Shit, maybe Sonny might slip into the lake and drown. I was open to anything.

He led me down to the beach where the Loon Lake trailhead was located. The opening was so narrow and covered over in vegetative growth, you wouldn't even know it existed if not for the wood sign nailed to a big birch tree, the words Loon Lake Trail embossed on it in big, bold white letters. Sonny stood at the trailhead and, holding the chainsaw in his right hand, yanked on the starter with his left. The saw came to life, its fat body spitting gas and oil, its chain trembling. Now holding the saw in both hands, he pressed the trigger, and the rapidly spinning chain came roaring to life. Raising the saw, he began to cut away the overgrown branches and twigs that concealed the trailhead. When he was done, he turned to me, his brow already beaded with sweat.

"Well, don't just stand there like a useless bump on a log, Oil and Gas Man," he said. "Pick that shit up."

He was, of course, referring to the pile of fresh lumber that now littered the beach.

"And do what with it exactly, boss?" I said, playing dumb.

"Jesus, you sure you're a writer?" he said over the sputtering noise of the idling saw. "'Cause you sure do come out with some dumb-ass questions."

"Sorry," I said, not without a smile. "City boy."

"Maybe that explains it," he said. Then, "Pick up the damned branches and toss them into the woods. Get it?"

The sun was coming up over the lake then, and now I could really make out his round face, along with the salt and pepper stubble and sweat that coated it. It seemed to glow in the early morning sunlight like a yellow lightbulb. The kind of lightbulb that attracted all sorts of flying insects. In fact, he looked like an insect to me. A big, hairy beetle with green goop for blood.

He stepped into the trees, began trudging along the trail, and I followed, the new morning sun now shaded by the foliage. Quickly, we came upon a tree that had come down over the winter, and he immediately started cutting it up.

I stood there holding the gas and oil cans and prayed that he would somehow lose control of the chainsaw on his own and it would cut into his leg, severing the femoral artery. I'd once seen a man die in Iraq after taking a bullet to the thigh. He bled out in just a few minutes. In the prison yard, I witnessed a repeat performance, only the poor bastard in this scenario was shanked in the thigh by another inmate. The cut was delivered so quickly and so deep, that the femoral artery had been sliced open and the poor bastard died within three minutes. By the time help arrived, he was lying in a pool of his own dark red blood, his eyes wide open, his soul having already departed his mortal remains.

The imaginary lightbulb illuminated over my head. As Sonny cut away at the felled tree, I found myself smiling. I knew now how I was going to kill him and how I was going to get away with it. The happiness and energy it filled me with was almost as good as typing The End on a new novel. Only this wasn't the end. It was just the beginning.

We proceeded deep into the woods, stopping every ten or twenty feet to cut away more branches and twigs or even to cut up an entire downed tree. By the time the first hour of work was history, we'd both worked up a sweat. Also, the chainsaw was out of both gas and oil. Now was my chance.

"You know what you're doing?" Sonny asked, referring to the chainsaw's gas and oil needs. He sat his big load down on the log he'd been cutting before the gas gave out, wiping his sweat-soaked brow with a gray handkerchief. "You just uncap each tank on the saw and ahhhh, you know, fill 'er up."

"Yup," I said, unscrewing the saw's gas cap. "I might be a city boy, but I grew up using a chainsaw on my dad's farm."

It was a lie I'd made up on the spot. My father...my stepfather, I should say...grew up in the burbs just like me. But what the hell was Sonny about to do? Question me? He was a gangster from Queens who only recently became a country caretaker. What did he really know about farming?

He pulled his vape device from his shirt pocket, took a long toke off it, and then returned it to his pocket.

"You don't say?" he said, exhaling the blue vapor. "You seem like all city boy to me."

"Not anymore," I said while I filled up the gas tank. "Now I'm all about Loon Lake, boss."

"Jeez," he went on, his eyes now focusing on the still lake through the breaks in the trees. "I should have brought some water along. It's already getting hot. Too hot for this early in the season. Must be that global warming shit all the libtards are always going on about. Can't say I believe in it much myself. But then, what the hell do I know? I'm just a simple caretaker now. A country gentleman who loves Loon Lake." He exhaled, wiped away more sweat. "You know, I'd love to see this place developed. Maybe a Hilton across the lake, a Sheraton beside it. Or shit, maybe even a Trump golf course. If only I could find a way to entice those companies— you know, present them with a solid business plan—there'd be millions to be made. Tens of millions. That little shithole of a village could become a bustling town, with a Gap, and a Starbucks, a McDonald's, a Red Robin, and maybe even an amusement park and a waterslide world. We'd have bars galore and high-end restaurants, and people would fly into our new airport just to shop at our retail outlets and our new mall." He wiped more sweat from his brow. "Fuck, Kingsley, maybe we could even get ourselves the Winter Olympic Games just like Lake Placid did back in 1980. Now, wouldn't that put this fucking backwater on the map? And it would make us filthy rich."

"Excuse me?" I said.

He laughed.

"Oh," he said. "Nothing."

Jesus, if I didn't know any better, I would have said that was Sonny's way of asking me to come work for him. Could be I was all wrong, but it seemed like he was presenting me with his business plan to take over Loon Lake in a roundabout way. He must have seen something in me. Some kind of talent. No wonder he hadn't confronted me about sleeping with his wife. No wonder he hadn't taken so much as a swipe at me.

I screwed the gas cap back on and then unscrewed the oil cap. Grabbing hold of the oil can, I began filling the chainsaw's oil tank.

"You'd have to buy out all the residents, I guess," I said as I was slowly filling the tank. "They might not want to leave their homes. This is their land, their property. Maybe they don't want to develop it."

He laughed like he was thinking of something very sinister, and he was.

"Oh, they'll move all right," he said. "You can trust me on that. They'll move out when they know what I have in store for them."

"So, you're buying up Loon Lake, boss?"

He pursed his lips like he'd slipped again. Like he was revealing too much information.

"Say, how you coming with reviving that saw, Gas and Oil Man?"

"Getting there," I said. Then, pointing at the lake, "Holy crap, look at the size of that bass jumping out of the water?"

Sonny immediately gazed at the lake over his shoulder.

"I don't see nothin'," he said.

That's when I dipped my hands in the oil and rubbed it all over the chain saw grip.

"You must have just missed it," I said. "Must have been a ten-pound largemouth."

Wiping the oil from my fingers on my jeans, I capped off the chainsaw oil reserve and placed the cap back on the oil can. Then I stepped away from the saw.

"All yours, boss," I said.

He put his gloves back on and picked up the saw with his left hand.

"It's heavier now," he said. "Feels a little slippery, too, like you got oil on it."

"That's probably just the sweat inside your gloves," I

said.

He yanked on the starter. The saw started up with a roar, but it was so slippery it dropped out of his hands and landed on the leaf-strewn trail.

"What the fuck," he said. "If that blade had been going, I might have lost a leg."

I reached down, retrieved the saw.

"You mean like this, boss?" I said, pressing my finger on the saw's trigger.

My eyes zeroing in on his left thigh, I pushed the screaming chainsaw against his thigh as if it was a pine log. I expected resistance, but the sharp blade sank through the flesh like a hot knife through the warmest butter. The blood spattered and shot out of the cut. There was so much blood, I knew I had not only connected with the artery but that I had severed it. I also knew that if I kept going, I would sever his leg completely, which would be a mistake. I had to make this look like Sonny did this by accident, all on his own. His natural, instinctual reaction would be to pull the blade out of his leg and drop the saw.

I yanked the blade out and tossed the saw to the ground. Sonny was just staring at me, his face growing paler by the second, the blood draining from his body through the open wound. How he was still standing was a miracle. His eyes wide open, he was moving his mouth, but not managing to say anything.

Until finally, he said, "What...did...you...do?" And then he collapsed like a sack of rags and bones.

What I did next, I had to do quickly. I had to make it look like Sonny not only managed to cut himself very badly, I had to make it look like I tried to save him...save him in vain, that is. He was on the ground, staring up at the brilliant blue sky. His leg was trembling while the blood spurted out of it. My mind raced. If this had been a real accident, how would I have handled it? I'd try to stop the bleeding. I'd do everything in my power to keep the son of a bitch from bleeding out and dying.

He was so pale his face looked like a white sheet. I could tell he was trying to say something to me. But the life was draining from him so fast, he didn't have the energy. He knew now that I had it out for him. He was dying with the knowledge that not only had I slept with his wife, I'd jammed that active chainsaw blade into his leg. He knew I'd been planning on killing him almost from the moment I met him, and that I hadn't hesitated to take my shot.

Still, I had to make it look good.

"Tourniquet," I whispered to myself. "He needs a tourniquet."

Bending over, I made a quick check to make sure he wasn't packing the semi-automatic. When I was sure he was unarmed, I untied his work boot and pulled the shoelace out of the eyelets. I wrapped the lace around his thigh, directly below the wound. I found a small stick, and I tied the ends of the lace to it. Then twisted it as hard as I could. Sonny wasn't as dead as I thought, let me tell you. He let loose with a scream that echoed across the lake and could be heard all the way down in Albany. Or so I was convinced.

But my efforts didn't stop the bleeding, nor did I want them to. Bleeding was a good thing. The more he hemorrhaged, the better. I bent down and tried to lift him up like I was thinking about carrying him out of the woods. That didn't work either. I dropped him. When he hit the ground, he let loose with a cry so pathetic and primal, I thought he was going to start crying.

"You...did...this," he said. "You...did it...on purpose. Because you love...my wife. Jesus, of all days to forget my piece. I'd blow your fucking brains out." He worked up a smile. It was crazy as hell because he was dying right in front of me, and he was smiling. "Well, you'll soon...find out...what Cora's all about. She's...no better...than me."

That little comment took me a little bit by surprise.

But maybe it was just the crazy banter of a dying man. No matter what, I had to be smart about this. What if he ended up living? I had to make it look like whatever happened out here in the woods of Loon Lake was just an accident, plain and simple. In the end, if he did live, it would be my word against his. An ex-con against a mobster/lawyer.

"Sonny…boss man," I said. "I'm surprised at you. Telling me I did this on purpose. Nothing could be further from the truth. It was an accident. I'm trying to save you now, aren't I?"

I gave the tourniquet another twist. He screamed again.

I was torturing him, and you know what? It felt good.

"I know…you were…fucking Cora in the cabin. Everybody wants to fuck Cora."

"Everybody, huh?" I said, hoping he'd take final breath sooner than later. "That's terrible, boss. How can you stand it?"

He smiled again, the red-black arterial blood pouring out of his leg like Niagara Falls.

"Looks like it won't be bothering me for much longer, asshole. If only you played your cards right…I could have…I could have…cut you in…cut you in on the action."

He was having real trouble talking now. Real trouble breathing. He was going in and out of consciousness, his entire body whiter than the ghost he was about to become "What action you talking about, boss?" I said. But I knew what he was going on about. My gut instincts had been right on. He wanted me to be a part of his team of gangsters.

"Loon Lake," he said. "It's ours."

I knew he didn't have long. Still, just in case he lived, I had to continue to make it look like I wanted to save his life. I squeezed the tourniquet again and again he screamed. Only this time, his voice was very weak. I was no doctor, but as a soldier, I was certain he was only minutes or even seconds from dying. Here's what else I knew as a soldier: the average male only had about six quarts of blood in him, and four of them had to be soaking the ground right now. Judging by the blood pool that was growing wider and wider with each passing second, I was convinced that his life was over. I wasn't sure why, but I didn't want to be around him when he exhaled that final breath.

"What do you mean it's yours?"

"The lake...the family...we're taking over the lake." He was telling me what I already knew. It was time for me to get the hell away from him, make it look like I was going for help. Because no way was I going to carry him the hell out of there.

"You keep talking, Sonny," I said, taking hold of his hand, placing it on the tourniquet. "And keep twisting this. I'm going for help."

"Be quick..." he said, his eyes now shut, his speech slurred. "I'm...dying."

I started back in the direction of the trailhead.

"Kingsley," he said, renewed energy in his voice.

I turned.

"Admit it. You were fucking her, weren't you?" He breathed in and out. "Last night in the cabin...I know the sound of her screams. I can smell my wife's pussy anywhere."

"Yeah, boss," I said. "I fucked her good."

What good would it do to lie at that point? Turning, I started down the path.

Vincent Zandri

16

I was never one for acting. One of my books had been optioned a few years back, and the B-level actor who financed it asked me if I wanted a bit part in the movie. That is, should it be lucky enough to actually get produced. I issued him a definitive no. Because no way was I about to make a fool of myself going out there on the big screen. But this situation was different. This time, I had to really make it look like I was one hell of an actor. The situation was the same for Cora.

I sprinted my way over the path, branches and twigs slapping me in the face, stinging it, making my eyes tear up. It was important to convince myself that Sonny had suffered a great accident. That I had nothing to do with it. That I wasn't the guy who purposely buried that chainsaw in his thigh, severing his femoral artery. It seemed to take forever to cover all that ground. There must have been a half mile or more separating Sonny and the trailhead at the beach.

But when I finally broke through, I shouted, "Cora! Cora! Come quick!"

She was nowhere to be found. I jogged over the sandy beach toward the tavern. I made my way around the building, up the front porch steps, and to the door. It was open. Barging inside, I shouted for Cora again. She came out of the office behind the counter.

"It's okay, Kingsley," she said. "You don't have to shout. There's nobody else here."

I thought about the parking lot. No other vehicles other than my Jeep and the pickup truck were parked there. No sheriff's prowler, no motorcycles, no strange cars or vans belonging to any guests. Of course, that's when it dawned on me. Maybe Loon Lake was never getting any visitors or guests. Maybe the place was just a front for the Torchi crime family.

"It's done," I said, looking her in the eyes.

She just stared at me for a minute. It wasn't a good stare. There was no enthusiasm in it. No hopefulness. No sign of relief. No love.

"Did you hear me, Cora?" I said. "It's done. He's cut bad."

She shook her head, as though to break herself out of her spell. Her eyes teared up.

"Oh my God," she said, "call an ambulance now!"

We called 911. It didn't take the EMT team very long to pull into the parking lot. And get this: the EMT team consisted, in part, of Bunny and the sheriff. Their sudden presence took me a bit by surprise when they both arrived in what I guessed was Loon Lake's only EMS van. But the sheriff and Bunny weren't alone. A young woman accompanied them.

Her name was Kate, and she was training with the team. Or so Sheriff Woods informed us.

The sheriff wasn't wearing the typical blue overall-like uniform most EMTs wore. Instead, he was wearing his usual uniform of jeans, boots, and black-and-red-checked shirt. He was also wearing his old cowboy hat, and his semi-automatic was strapped to his hip.

"What happened?" he asked me, his face straight, his demeanor calm and cool.

I told him all about Sonny's accident. How he'd cut himself bad with the chainsaw.

"Holy fuck," Bunny said, her face lit up like a lantern. "If he hit the femoral, he's as good as dead already."

That's when Cora started weeping. The tears were streaming down her face. If she was acting, and I could only pray that she was, she was doing one hell of a job of it.

"We don't know that, Bun," the sheriff said. "Blood can coagulate. Wounds can scab and heal themselves given the right conditions."

"That's right, Sheriff," Kate said while brushing back her shoulder-length sandy blonde hair. "The body does everything it can to heal itself, even when badly cut."

I felt ice water speed through my veins. What if Sonny were still alive? What then? Better to not think about that right now. Because no way the Sonny I left out there on the trail was still going to be alive when we got to him. If it were just Bunny and the sheriff heading out to tend to him and he were alive, I wasn't sure either person would have had an issue with us finishing the job off. Sonny and his entire family of mobsters were the enemies of Loon Lake after all. The sheriff wanted Sonny dead as much as Cora and I did. But with this girl, Kate, in tow, I knew we'd have no choice but to play things straight, no matter what we found along the trail…dead or alive.

"Follow me," I said, leading everyone to the beachside trailhead.

Kate grabbed hold of the big plastic portable medical kit. The other two followed on her tail while Cora decided to stay back at the tavern.

"I can't bear to see him like this," she said.

I told her I understood and that we'd do everything in our power to see that her husband survived the ordeal. Like

I said, we were acting, playing our separate roles. If all went well, at the end of this movie would be one very dead Sonny Torchi.

"How far in is he?" Kate asked as we entered the dark forest.

"About a half mile," I said. "Give or take. We need to take it double-time."

She was young and enthusiastic. She was pretty, too. A part of me was really attracted to her. I guess you could say I even felt the urge to kiss her, right off the bat. But that wasn't a good sign, considering I might have just committed murder, or, at the very least, attempted murder on behalf of my love for Cora. Love and lust. How's that old Doors song go again? People are strange?

"I love your take-charge attitude, Mr. Kingsley," she said, that medical box gripped in her hand. "You're obviously worried."

But I wasn't worried. I was, instead, imagining what it would be like to be with her. What she would feel like with me inside her. Turning, I headed into the woods.

I didn't want to appear panicked, but I didn't want to make myself look like I was taking Sonny's imminent demise with a grain of sea salt either. That said, I took the lead as we negotiated the narrow trail. Sonny and I had made serious progress on them during the couple hours we'd spent clearing them, so the going wasn't all that hard. The newly sawed away branches and felled birch and pine trees that had once blocked the path were now cut away, making the hiking a breeze. Maybe too much of a breeze.

What if the son of bitch wasn't dead yet?

The obvious decision was, of course, to slow things down. Take half steps where full steps would have been the easy and logical thing to do. The natural thing.

After about twenty minutes, Sheriff Woods barked

out, "How much longer, Kingsley?"

"Yeah," Bunny added, "I'm sweatin' so much right now I could go for a beer."

"Are we close?" Kate asked, genuine concern in her pretty voice.

"A little longer," I said. "Maybe another ten minutes."

"He'll be bled out by then," Bunny said. "I'm telling you, stone fucking dead."

"Don't be so negative, Bunny," Kate said. "He could very well be alive but in real danger nonetheless. Our job is to get to him as quickly as possible."

"Who died and left her boss?" Bunny said. "She's just a kid."

"And doing a very fine job," Woods added. "Just keep hiking, Bun."

Wiping the sweat from my brow, I knew we were getting close. In a minute or two, I'd be able to see the very spot where I left Sonny lying in a big puddle of his own blood. I couldn't get it out of my head that he'd be somehow sitting up, a smile plastered on his face. He'd be toking on his vape device, blue steam oozing from his nostrils. The bleeding would have stopped due to the tourniquet I rigged up, and even his color would have returned. Sure, he'd need stitches and lots of them, but otherwise, he would be no worse for wear.

He'd go wide-eyed when he saw the sheriff.

"Well, ain't I glad to see you, Sheriff Woods," he'd say. "Boy, have I got a story for you." Then he'd take special notice of me, too. "And our new writer boy, Kingsley, can help me tell it. Can't you, Kingsley?"

That was the problem with being a writer. You couldn't help but let your imagination run wild. You couldn't help but imagine all the possibilities of any given situation, good or really bad. It was a matter of instinct. It was great for the work. But it also was also the reason why I was able to survive a joint like Sing Sing for as long as I did. I was always playing out different scenarios in my mind. Would a beefy, skin-headed Aryan sneak up on me in the showers and shiv me in the kidney with a sharpened toothbrush? Would a big black stud corner me, make me get down on my knees, make me give him what he wanted with my mouth and tongue while a screw turned his back on the whole thing? Or maybe a riot would break out in the mess hall. Maybe the plastic trays and the cups would start flying, and the whole place would explode, and it would be everyone for himself. The screws would run for their lives, and there would be no one to protect anyone. The Aryans had gotten to me once, when I wasn't imagining the bad things that could happen to me.

Day in and day out, I imagined the worst, and it was those thoughts that kept me on my toes at all times. They kept me alive. But now, I was imagining something completely different. I had just attempted murder, and I couldn't be sure that I'd done the job properly. When I'd left Sonny behind, I'd been super confident that he was a goner. Now I wasn't so sure. The sweat that was building up under my clothing and the sweat that was beading on my face wasn't just from the onset of a hot day. It was also because of my nerves.

I didn't get nervous very often. When you lived in a state of constant anxiety, you learned not to sweat the little things in life. But if it ended up that Sonny survived, I'd be looking at a court-mandated lethal injection or, at the very least, life behind bars, which in itself was an agonizingly slow death.

Breathing shallow, heart pumping in my throat, I pushed back some branches that concealed the spot where I'd left Sonny Torchi, bleeding out. My stomach dropped when I saw that he was gone.

17

A massive pool of blood soaked the leafy ground directly beside the pine log he'd been cutting when the chainsaw ran out of gas. I looked one way and then the other. I spotted the chainsaw set on the trail bed. But no Sonny. Kate approached me. So did the sheriff and Bunny.

"Is this the place?" Kate said, her eyes wide, her pretty face having barely worked up a sweat.

"Yes," I said. "I swear I left him right here. That's his blood."

"Well, then, he can't be dead, can he?" Woods said.

"Well, I'll be a dumb-ass broad," Bunny said, not without a hoarse laugh. "That son of a bitch must have had some life left in him after all."

My throat went dry. The fine hairs on the back of my neck stood up. Was Bunny right? Had Sonny somehow managed to get up and walk into the woods even with most of his body bled out? What the hell was happening here? No way Sonny could have gotten up and walked away. Not in the condition he was in. I stared at the ground. It took a few beats, but soon I saw something that looked different from everything else. There was a smear of blood that ran from the blood pool, off the trail and into the thick woods.

"Maybe he tried to crawl his way out," I said, pointing at the long blood trail.

"Looks like it to me," Kate said, her eyes now focused on the same blood smear.

The sheriff locked eyes with me. His eyes were steely gray, his face long, cheeks concave, his upper lip invisible under that salt and pepper mustache. I'm not sure why he felt the need to do it, but he drew his gun.

"Expecting company?" Bunny said.

"I got a funny feeling," Sheriff Woods said. Then, his eyes still locked on mine, "Kingsley, you'd better let me take the lead from here on out. Understand?"

My temples were pounding in time with my pulse. I might have been covered in sweat, but I had goose pimples.

"Follow me," the sheriff said.

I swallowed something dry and bitter tasting and did what he said.

"Try not to walk so loud," Woods went on as he followed the blood trail.

"Do as he says," Kate whispered. "Sheriff Woods knows his woods, if you get my drift."

I did.

"When we finally find Torchi," Bunny said, "drinks are on me back at the bar."

"One thing at a time, Bunny," the sheriff said. "Let's find Sonny first and take it from there."

It grunted at us through the trees. A deep, angry, guttural grunt that sent a shiver through my bones.

"Stand back," Woods demanded in a shouting whisper.

He took careful aim with his weapon, slowly cocked

back the hammer. He fired. There came another grunt. This one agonized. Until the grunting suddenly stopped and we made out a heavy thump on the forest floor.

"Dead on," Woods said, not without a grin. He turned. "Bunny, radio in that I just shot a black bear on the Loon Lake Trail and that Encon is gonna have to come pick it up." He holstered his pistol. "Oh, and tell them I want the hide. I don't care if black bear season isn't for five months yet."

My head was spinning with the possibilities. Was this the black bear Sonny had mentioned yesterday? The one with the tag in the ear? The one Encon had sent a warning about? Had that same black bear actually sniffed out Sonny's blood just like a hungry shark would sniff out the blood of a mortally wounded fish or even a human being? But then Kate asked the question that had to be on everyone's minds.

"Sheriff," she said, "did the bear take Torchi's body?"

"You people stay back," he said. "Judging by the direction of the blood trail, that's exactly what's happened. I've heard of this kind of thing happening before, especially with wounded hunters stupid enough to shoot themselves in the feet with their own guns. Or occasionally, one of their hunting partners will confuse them for a deer. A man gets shot, collapses in the woods, and the bears take over. It's like a shooting gallery out here in November and December."

He started toward the shot bear. I followed.

"Stay back, Kingsley," he said, again drawing his gun. "That bear might still be alive."

He walked into the woods. His bootsteps crushing and crunching the dead leaves that covered the forest floor.

When I could barely see him, he shouted, "The bear is dead!"

"What about Torchi?" Kate barked.

"He's here all right," he said. "He don't look so good. Hang on while I check his vitals."

"What are we waiting for?" Bunny said, now jogging her way to the sheriff with Kate following close on her boot heels.

"Holy shit," Woods called out. "He's alive. Sonny Torchi has a pulse."

My worst fears were confirmed. How the hell did a man bleed out, then get snatched up by a black bear, get dragged into the woods, and live through the ordeal? If I were to write this kind of thing in a novel, my editor would tell me it was unbelievable, that my plot and storyline had somehow gone radically off the rails. But like they say, you can't make this shit up. Or what's the other one…truth is all too often stranger than fiction.

I made my way to the scene and nearly puked over what I witnessed. Sonny was on his back, his mouth wide open, white foam oozing out both corners, his blue tongue sticking out like an insult. His eyes were open wide and every now and again he'd wink, as if he were sending me a personal message in Morse Code: "I'm alive, you cocksucker, and I know what you did, and now you're a fucking dead man."

The dead black bear was lying right beside him, a small trickle of blood running from its head down over its snout. Its left ear had a yellow Encon tag stuck to it. The bear smelled like shit, let me tell you. I had to admit, Woods had made one hell of a shot. A headshot. The sheriff knew how to shoot, that was for sure. Take it from a soldier who proudly earned his marksmanship medal. Apparently, the bear hadn't dug its teeth into Sonny's skin, but instead just managed to drag him along the forest floor by his bloody pant leg. Too bad the bear hadn't bitten him in the neck.

The others hadn't quite reached the site yet, so I whispered to Woods, "What the hell do we do now? The bastard's alive."

He took hold of my arm.

"Not for long," he said. His voice was so low, it wasn't even a whisper. I practically had to lip read him.

"I need that one-hundred grand, Sheriff," I said.

"You'll get it when he's gone, and when the town is safe from his family."

He was right, of course. That's exactly the way I'd handle the money portion of our program if I were in his boots. The others broke through the brush.

"How is he?" Kate asked.

She immediately dropped to her knees, tossing the medical kit down beside her. She pressed the left side of her head against Sonny's chest, her ear against his heart.

Bunny just stood there staring at the dying man.

"Think I'm gonna barf," she said.

"Bunny!" Sheriff Woods barked. "Come on, have more respect than that."

She locked eyes with him. "You're kidding, Sheriff, right? We all know what Sonny is."

Woods just shook his head and bit down on his lip. Kate was present, so he knew, like I knew, that he had to go through all the motions of saving the caretaker's life.

"Think you can stabilize him, Kate?" he said. "He's too far bled out for my skills. And no way are we're choppering him out in these heavily forested conditions."

"I'm gonna give it my best," Kate said, opening the kit, grabbing a hold of some medical scissors.

She proceeded to cut away Sonny's blood and mud-stained shirt and then the pant leg that covered the gaping wound caused by the chainsaw.

"Bunny," she said, "don't just stand there. Take care of his tongue."

"Yeah, yeah, yeah," Bunny said, her tone indicating that all this fuss would be for nothing.

I couldn't only hope she was right.

Reaching into the kit, Bunny came out with a plastic device which she placed over Sonny's blue tongue. Presumably, so he didn't swallow it or choke on it. Meanwhile, Kate slipped on some blue latex gloves and then went to work on the massive gash in Sonny's leg. It was still bleeding, but not nearly as much as it had been when I first left him.

"I need to clamp this off," Kate said. "Sheriff, can you pass me two clamps?"

Woods took a knee, found the clamps, and handed them to her.

"Sonny," she said, "if you can hear me, this is gonna hurt bad." Then, looking up at me, "Mr. Kingsley, I need you to hold down Mr. Torchi's shoulders. He's liable to make a fuss when I apply the clamps."

"Sure," I said. What the hell else could I say?

I stepped over to where his head was set on the forest floor. Taking a knee just like Woods had before me, I pressed my hands on both his shoulders and put my weight into it.

"Here we go," Kate said.

When she stuck the first clamp deep into the wound and snapped it shut on the severed artery, Sonny heaved his chest into the air. He also yelped like a dog. He gave off the same reaction when she clamped the other half of the severed artery. He coughed up more foamy phlegm, and then he seemed to pass out again.

"Is he dead?" Bunny asked.

Kate took hold of Sonny's left hand, felt his pulse.

"He's just fainted is all," she said. "But his pulse is almost nonexistent. We need to get him out of here." She looked between the sheriff and me. "We can wait for someone to bring us a stretcher or we can all chip in to carry him out of here."

"Oh, for God's sakes," Bunny said. "He's, like, three-hundred pounds."

Kate reached back inside the medical kit, pulled out a syringe. She filled the syringe with clear fluid from a vial. I could only guess that it was an antibiotic. When she was done, she tossed the syringe back into the kit, closed it, and stoodup.

"He needs blood and saline, stat," she said. "We carry him, or he dies."

The Caretaker's Wife

"Okay," Sheriff Woods said, clearly playing along. "Let's do this. Kingsley, you're the strong man here. You take the shoulders, and I'll take the legs. Ladies, you take the arms."

He then indicated that we all lift on three. I never thought deadweight could be so heavy. Maybe he wouldn't make it out of the woods after all.

"What about the medical kit?" Bunny asked.

"I can carry it with my free hand," Kate said, bending at the knees and grabbing hold of it.

We started for the trail, straining our backs on behalf of a man who was better off dead.

Vincent Zandri

18

By the time we made it back to the trailhead at the Loon Lake beach, we were all exhausted and soaking in our own sweat. Cora was there to greet us, the tears still streaming down her face.

"Oh my God!" she screamed. "Is my husband dead?" Her roleplaying was spot on. So spot on, it made me sick to my stomach. Or maybe by then, the whole morning was making me sick to my stomach.

"He's not dead," Bunny said. "So stop with the dramatics already."

"Bunny!" Sheriff Woods barked. "That will be enough."

Bunny went sort of pale then.

"My apologies, Mrs. Torchi," she said. "Been a long morning. We'll take good care of your husband."

But I knew Bunny was hoping that he'd die as much as me, Woods, and Cora were hoping he'd die. We all had our own reasons for wanting Sonny dead, but taken collectively, they all added up to one thing: Torchi was a bad man with bad people under his employ and even badder gangsters propping him up down in Queens. There was something else to consider. If he survived this ordeal, it could very well mean that I'd have to find another way to kill him and do it quickly, before he opened his trap and spilled everything.

I went to Cora, wrapped my arms around her, not like her new boyfriend, but a very concerned friend. She cried and trembled in my arms. After a time, she placed her lips near my ear.

"What are we going to do?" she said. "He's still alive." My heart began to speed up, and my body felt suddenly lighter than air. Cora had been putting on a terrific act after all.

"I'll take care of it," I said. "I promise."

"Will you go to the hospital?"

"Yes," I said. "Do you want me to drive you?"

"That would be the right thing," she said.

While Bunny, Kate, and the sheriff piled into the EMS van, Cora and I got into my Jeep. I fired it up, and we followed the speeding van out the gravel drive and onto Loon Lake Road, which would take us through the town and to Crown Point General. While the warm wind slapped our faces, Cora remained silent. It was as if she were waging a war against herself. On one hand, she wanted her husband dead. Wanted him dead more than anything in the world. On the other hand, she was a good person. And good people didn't take murder with a casual grain or two of salt. Just the thought of carrying out the act would cause enough turmoil in their heads and bodies to twist up their intestines and mess up their brains.

I knew Cora was fighting that very war because I could see it in her eyes. The way they hardly blinked. The way her million-mile stare saw far beyond the road and the mountains and the trees. Maybe she hadn't been the one to cut her husband in the thigh, but she was just as guilty as I was. Maybe more so. And she knew it in her flesh and bones, and most of all, in her heart and soul.

We cruised through town, past the jail, past the grocery store, past the burned house, past Bunny's bar, and past all the old houses falling apart from both lack of repair and lack of money.

Maybe Torchi was a creep who deserved to die, but one thing was for sure, the town of Loon Lake sure could use a facelift. As soon as the town was behind us, I set my hand on Cora's leg. But she pushed it off. She turned to me.

"Don't," she said. "Not now. Not for a long time. We must be strong."

Her voice was somewhat drowned out by the wind, but I heard her all right. She wanted to be left alone. Even in the presence of someone who loved her so much he'd kill for her, she wanted only to be left alone. I guess I couldn't blame her one bit.

I kept my mouth shut and my hands to myself for the rest of the drive to Crown Point.

The EMS van pulled up to the emergency drop off at Crown Point General. Two orderlies dressed in blue scrubs came running out, opened the back door on the van, and pulled the stretcher out. They immediately wheeled Sonny into the emergency room. The EMS van pulled ahead. I drove up to the emergency drop off. Cora got out and went in through the automatic sliding glass doors. Then I parked the Jeep in an empty parking space only a few feet away from the still idling van. Shutting off the engine, I got out.

That's when Woods approached me.

"Bunny and Kate will take the EMS van back to the jail," he said. "It needs to be available in case of another emergency." Bunny and Kate got out, leaving the van doors open. My eyes shifted to Kate.

"Thanks for your good work, Kate," I lied. "We couldn't have saved him without you."

"Yeah, you're welcome," Bunny jumped in.

"You too, Bunny," I added.

"If he lives," she said, "it will be a miracle. Either way, I wanna treat everyone to a drink later."

"We'll be there," Woods said.

But I couldn't help but wonder if that was Bunny's way of calling a meeting of the minds. Because even if Sonny didn't make it, his family would be sending up reinforcements. And those reinforcements would be an army to be reckoned with. Bunny got back behind the wheel of the EMS van, and Kate hopped back up into the shotgun seat. Closing the doors, Bunny took off for the parking lot exit. Sheriff Woods turned to me.

"You realize he cannot live," he said.

"That's all I've been thinking about since his, ummm, accident."

"Either way, the Torchis are gonna send in the troops, and when they do, it's gonna be ugly."

"How do you propose we proceed, Sheriff?"

He bit down on his bottom lip. Both his thumbs stuffed into his leather belt, he said, "My guess is he doesn't make it through the day. But just in case, we'll keep a close eye on him for now."

His words somehow made me feel better.

"Shall we go in and pretend like we're pulling for him?" I asked.

"Wouldn't you?" he said.

He started for the emergency room. I followed, knowing that I had mortally wounded Sonny Torchi. But I'll be damned if he wasn't taking a long time to die.

As soon as we got inside the big white room, we saw the team of medical professionals frantically working on Sonny. He'd been transferred from the gurney to a stainless steel table. His shirt and pants were now completely removed, and only a green sheet covered his privates. A bag of blood and another of saline were being mainlined into his system via an IV that was needled into the thick blue vein on the back of his left hand. A spaghetti of wires were hooked up to him. One or two of those wires were hooked up to a flat-screen television monitor that had an electronic green line running through it. Every now and then the green line would rise up like a snake slithering its way through the tall grass. It told me Sonny's stubborn heart was still beating.

But then something happened. Something wonderful. The green line fell flat, and a loud buzzer sounded.

"Defibrillator paddles," a young doctor dressed in the same green scrubs shouted. "Paddles now, dammit!"

"Hold your horses, Doctor," one of the nurses scolded. She was short, with shoulder-length auburn hair.

"We've got a flat line, Doris," Young Doctor said. "Don't you ever tell me to hold my horses again!"

She applied some clear jelly to two white paddles that were attached to a portable defibrillator machine. She handed the paddles to Young Doctor. Sonny's big, white, blood-smeared belly was shaking like Jell-O as Young Doctor pressed the two paddles to his chest and shouted, "Clear!" There was an explosion, and the caretaker's body nearly jumped off the gurney. Every medical professional surrounding the gurney focused their eyes on the green line then, waiting for it to rise up in an arc. But it never happened.

"Again," Young Doctor insisted.

You should have seen the doc's face. It was almost as white as Sonny's. It gave me the feeling he'd never lost a man before. Not on his watch anyway. The nurse prepared the paddles again. She handed them over.

"Clear!"

Young Doctor triggered the paddles and Sonny jumped again, but not as high this time. The green line stayed flat, too. That annoying buzz filled the otherwise empty ER, and all I wanted was for it to stop. The son of bitch was dead already. Couldn't they see that?

I glanced at Woods. He shot me a glance in return that was so stone cold, it made me shiver. But it was nothing to be worried about. On the contrary, it was an expression that conveyed victory.

"Fuck!" Young Doctor shouted. "We're gonna open him up. Get him ready."

"Doctor," Doris said. "You really think it's necessary? He's gone. We should just call it."

"I've haven't lost a patient before, and I'm not about to start now."

As if God were listening to Young Doctor, the green line moved. The flatline turned into an arc.

"We've got a pulse!" Young Doctor shouted.

His eyes were wide like he was Dr. Frankenstein giving life to a man put together from a whole bunch of spare body parts. I felt my mouth go dry and my stomach drop to somewhere around my ankles. I shot a look at Woods, but he wouldn't look back at me. He was entirely focused on Sonny.

I took a step forward toward Sonny. It was almost as if my gut was telling me to just kill him off once and for all. But that was ridiculous and the stuff of fantasy. What wasn't fantasy was when Torchi opened his eyes, turned his head, and stared right at me. He opened his mouth then and mumbled something. It sounded like he was saying, "Him… him…him." But his energy was entirely sapped, and it was impossible to understand precisely what he was trying to say. Or maybe I was fooling myself. Because I knew exactly what he was trying to say. He was trying to say I killed him. He was pointing the finger at me.

When the line went flat again and the alarm sounded, I felt only relief. He was dead again, and God willing, dead he would stay.

"We're gonna open him up," Young Doctor insisted.

"You're sure?" Doris asked.

"I'm gonna open him," Young Doctor said while pulling on a fresh pair of latex gloves.

The Caretaker's Wife

What followed was a quick series of injections pumped directly into Sonny's chest. Then, Young Doctor made a long, deep, vertical incision that began at the top of Sonny's clavicle and ended down by his stomach. The doctor glanced at Woods and me over his shoulder.

"If you two don't want to stay for this, I'll understand," he said. "It isn't very pretty."

"We're staying," Woods said.

"I'm ex-military," I said. "I've seen worse, believe me."

Young Doctor then split the clavicle open using a small hand saw. Blood was spraying everywhere. It was like a horror flick that, despite the brutal things I'd seen on the battlefield, made my stomach feel bad. It was a cruel procedure to witness, but Sheriff Woods and I were glued to it like a kid might be glued to a violent video game. When Sonny's chest was split open, Young Doctor reached in and began to massage the dead caretaker's heart, as if the act would somehow resurrect him. He must have massaged the heart for five minutes until finally, he let go of it. Making a fist with his blood covered hand, he pounded it on the table.

"Goddammit!" he screamed.

"You did everything you possibly could, Doctor," Doris said. "Don't be so hard on yourself."

Young Doctor removed his latex gloves, tossed them into a blue biowaste bin.

"Call and record the time of death, Doris," he said. Then, glancing at us, "Sorry I couldn't save him, Sheriff. He was just too bled out. The shock of it all was too much."

Woods and I both feigned sullen expressions. "We appreciate everything you did for Mr. Torchi, Doctor," the sheriff said. "I'll alert his wife ASAP." He said ASAP like it was a word.

I simply nodded. My eyes were glued to Sonny's split open chest...his exposed lungs and heart. It was hard to believe this was the same man who was playing saxophone a couple nights ago, and who held a gun on his wife and me.

His death was still not quite sinking in. But he was dead all right. What did Hemingway once say about death? The dead look really dead when they're dead. I'd seen plenty of it on the battlefield, which is why I wasn't shocked at the sight of Sonny's mutilated body so much as sickened, if not a little bit saddened. Seemed a shame it all had to come down to this.

But on the bright side of things, now I would not only have Cora to myself, I would be that much closer to my promised one-hundred K. And no way in hell was I going to jail. The only witness to my cutting Sonny Torchi in the thigh with a chainsaw and opening up his femoral artery was now fast on his way to hell. I could only hope the devil was waiting for him with open arms.

19

I was driving Woods back to Loon Lake. He was quiet for most of the ride until he cleared his throat and ran both hands over his face.

"I don't know how you managed to pull off what you did this morning on the Loon Lake Trail, and I'm not going to ask you how you did it. It was an accident, and when you're dealing with chainsaws, bad accidents are bound to happen from time to time. That's all this was, and that's all I need to know. I'm just forever grateful it happened."

"What about my one-hundred-thousand, Sheriff Grateful?" I asked, pressing the issue.

He was quiet again for a long beat. I felt the wind blowing against my face and against my hair. I knew that Woods's brain was spinning right now. Sonny Torchi might be dead and gone but that didn't mean our problems were solved.

"They're going to come after us," he said after a time. "When they find out Sonny is dead, they're going to assume we somehow killed him."

"Why would they assume that?" I asked, playing devil's advocate. "Like you said, it was an accident."

"Big Billy knows you were clearing the trail with Sonny. He doesn't like you, doesn't trust you. He knows you have eyes for Sonny's wife. He'll call bullshit on the accident theory and suspect you of murdering his boss."

I recalled the spaghetti and meatballs dinner Sonny and his crew of biker goons enjoyed last night. I was sure my name came up more than once, and when it did, it wasn't just casual conversation.

"They're going to come after us hard," Woods went on.

"So, what are you getting at?"

"I want you to help us defend Loon Lake," he said. "When we've beaten the bastards back…when they've given up…the money is yours."

The sheriff promised me one-hundred grand if I took care of Sonny and helped him save Loon Lake from some pretty bad gangsters down in New York City. I'd completed half the task set out for me. Completed it for him, for Loon Lake, and most of all, for Cora. I felt I deserved something for my efforts.

"I'll take half now," I said. "Or you're on your own."

He nodded and bit down on his lip again. "Okay," he said. "I guess that's only fair. I'll work up the cash for you by tomorrow."

We were quiet for a time while the town of Loon Lake appeared on the horizon.

"The state police will make an inquiry into Sonny's death," I said. It was a question.

"Almost certainly," he said. "They'll be angry that their cash cow is deceased. If they show up, just tell them the truth the way you see it. Let's get them out of our hair as quickly as humanly possible."

"Understood," I said. "And my parole officer?" Slowing the Jeep, I pulled into the jail parking lot, stopped, threw the transmission into park.

"I'll call him as soon as I get inside," he said. "I'll give him a full report on your employment and, naturally, the tragedy that went down this morning. I'll tell him all about your heroic efforts to try to save your new employer. He'll want you to call him directly sooner than later, but I think I can keep him at bay for you, for now."

"So then," I said, "how shall I proceed?"

"Go back to Loon Lake Inn. Let Cora know about her husband. Stay close to her. We'll all meet up at Bunny's at seven tonight. Make a plan." He opened the door, got out, and turned to me. "There will be a funeral. People will come up from New York. Bad people. They will be the ones who we will eventually have to face down. The ones who will want to take our town. You understand?"

I nodded.

"This isn't my town," I said. "But with all due respect, my guess is they won't wait until the funeral is over to hit us."

"You keep telling yourself this isn't your town, Kingsley," he said. "But you've got skin in the game now whether you wanna believe it or not. You've got Sonny's blood on your hands and your head wrapped around his widow's heart. And you just might be right about the war starting sooner than later."

"Guess I couldn't have written that bit of dialogue any better," I said.

"You'll get half your money soon as I can work it up," he said. "When this town is secure, you get the rest. Hell, you might even get to be the new caretaker of Loon Lake Inn."

"Now, wouldn't that be something," I said.

"Stranger things," the sheriff said.

"Stranger things," I said.

Backing out, I pulled out onto the road and headed for a dead reckoning with Cora.

She was sitting on the porch steps of the tavern when I

pulled in. Her face was pale and withdrawn, and I sensed the gravity of what I had done to her husband this morning was only now settling in. I parked the Jeep and went to her. She stood up and surprised the hell out of me when she wrapped her arms around me and held me so tight I thought my back might break. I wanted to kiss her. But I knew that would be the wrong thing to do.

She released me, wiped the tears from her eyes.

"Was he at peace?" she asked.

I recalled his coming back to life for a brief second. Long enough to call me out on his murder. "Him… him…him…"

"He never regained consciousness," I lied.

"That's a good thing, I suppose," she said.

"You're free now, Cora," I said. "You and me…we're free to be together."

She looked into my eyes. "Then why do I want to be alone?"

"That will change," I said. "You have a funeral to arrange. I'll help you as much as I can."

Her face went ghost white. "His family must be notified," she said. "They won't like what happened. They'll want to get to the bottom of it."

"The sheriff and I are ready for that. We're ready for the state police, too. They'll make an inquiry. But like Woods already said, accidents happen with chainsaws all the time."

"That might appease the state police," she said. "But it won't satisfy Sonny's family. They already know how much the residents of Loon Lake hated him."

"Mind if I ask you something personal, Cora?"

"You just killed my husband," she said, not without a bitter laugh. "How much more personal can it get?"

Her comments caused a tightness in my sternum.

"Did Sonny have any life insurance?"

She shook her head.

"He might have had a small policy on behalf of the

180

inn and the tavern, but it wasn't for much. Sonny has family money. Dirty money. Gangster money. He never felt the need for life insurance."

"How are you set for cash?" I asked.

"I have a little," she said. "It will cover the expenses of the funeral. His family will chip in. They're worth more than God."

"I'm about to run into a little cash myself," I said. "Listen, don't take a dime from Sonny's family. You don't want to be beholden to them. Just pay for it on your own. I'll help."

She nodded. "Guess I better get inside and call the funeral parlor in Crown Point."

That's when we heard the thunder. But it wasn't coming from the sky. It was coming from three Harley Davidson motorcycles speeding up the gravel drive.

Big Billy was riding point as usual. The other two followed close behind. Also, per usual, they were dressed in black leather. He pulled right up to the porch steps and came to a skidding stop. He dismounted while pulling off his black, imitation Nazi Germany motorcycle helmet. Slowly, he approached us.

"Billy," I said not without a bright smile. "So, how's your day going, buddy?"

His face was round and covered with stubble. If I didn't know any better, I'd say he'd been crying. His two amigos were still seated on their bikes, the engines idling like angry tigers.

"I'm awfully sorry for your loss, Cora," he said. "I loved your husband. You know that."

Cora sniffled. She was back to acting like the grieving widow, and for very good reason. Big Billy was one of Sonny's top men. Maybe the on-the-take state police were about to come calling at any moment, seeking out the truth to what happened in the woods along the Loon Lake Trail. But Big Billy wouldn't be concerned with the truth, so much as he'd want revenge. Sonny's entire family would want revenge.

"Mind if I have a word with Mr. Kingsley here alone, Cora?" he said.

I felt my stomach tighten and my built-in danger detector start up. Cora gave me a look like, be careful. But I think she knew I could handle myself better than most. She and the sheriff knew how good I could handle myself. How capable a survivor I really was. It was the reason they both wanted me to get rid of Sonny. Only I could make it happen. Only I had the guts.

"I need to head inside and start making some calls," she said, her voice cracking.

Turning, she made her way up the few steps to the porch and then into the tavern. She had a difficult series of tasks ahead of her. I didn't envy her one bit. But I did love her like no other.

Standing foursquare, I locked onto Billy's eyes. "What's on your mind, Bill?" I asked. "Besides lunch, of course."

He extended his index finger and poked my chest with it. It felt like the fat end of a pool cue. It was also enough to turn on the rage machine inside my soul. But if there was one important lesson I took away from both prison and the battlefield, it was this: you had to learn when to make the rage work for you, and more importantly, you had to learn when to rein it in. Right now, I had to rein it in.

I gazed down at his finger, then slowly, I raised my head, looked him in the eyes.

"I don't know what the hell went down in them woods," he said, his voice deep and gruff. "All I know is my boss is dead, and you were with him when he cut his leg so bad he bled out."

"What might you be insinuating, Bill?" I said, my tone jovial, mocking. "Or do I need to define the word insinuating for you? It's a derivative of insinuation if that helps."

He worked up a wad of phlegm and spat it on the

ground.

"You keep it up, funny man," he said. "You're already on my shit list." He glanced over his shoulder at his two gangster sidekicks. "Our shit list, I should say."

"Now I'm like, really, really scared, Bill," I said. "I might have to change my underwear."

He extended his index finger again, but he came just a hair short of touching my chest with it. If he had, I would have broken it on the spot. By then, the rage was building up like the fire in a blast furnace, and he knew it too. He could maybe see it in my eyes that I wasn't a man to fool around with. He'd already learned the hard way in Bunny's parking lot. He had no choice but to act tough in front of his crew.

"I'm gonna find out what happened, Kingsley," he said. "With Sonny gone, I'm the boss around here until they find someone else to take over this territory."

"And who would they be?" I said. "I thought Sonny was the simple caretaker of a simple country inn. You make it sound like he might be a part of the mob or a crime family or something nefarious like that." Extending my index finger, this time it was me who poked him in his barrel chest. "It dawns on me that you probably don't know what nefarious means."

He tried to slap my finger away but I was too quick for him, and instead, I grabbed hold of his hand. He tried to move it, but it was like trying to bend steel. Did I need to mention my twenty-month stint in prison, Big Bill? The hours I spent on the Sing Sing rec yard weightlifting platform? Just then, there was the sound of a car coming up the drive. Big Bill's hand was still gripped in my own when the car entered the lot. It wasn't just a car but a very special car. It was a yellow and blue New York State Trooper cruiser.

I released Big Bill's hand while he gazed at the cruiser over his shoulder.

"Shit," he said.

"What's wrong, Bill?" I said. "Something to hide? Like the way you and your boys have been extorting the residents and business owners? The way you've been harassing them, threatening them with physical violence? And what about the family you burned to death? You afraid of the staties not because they want the truth, but because the dude who's been signing their checks is dead? Who's gonna pay them now. You?"

"Fuck you, Kingsley," he said. "We'll continue this conversation later on, you hear me?"

"Loud and crystal," I said.

The cruiser parked between my Jeep and Cora's pickup. The trooper got out. He was a large African American man. He placed his Stetson on his head and approached the porch.

"Good afternoon," he said, placing his fingertips to the rim of his hat like John Wayne would do in a movie while saying howdy. "I'm looking for Mrs. Torchi and Mr. Jonathan Kingsley."

"I'm Kingsley," I said.

"I'm Lieutenant Otis Spenser. I'm investigating the recent death of Mr. Sonny Torchi." He glanced at Big Bill, then back at me. "You have somewhere we can talk in private, Mr. Kingsley?"

"Certainly," I said, my pulse speeding up enough for me to know I had to tread lightly with this state cop. Sure, he could very well be one of the bad ones. But he could be one of the legit ones, too. "My friends were just leaving. Isn't that right, Bill buddy?"

Big Bill turned and without a word, remounted his bike. He kick-started the Harley to life, and for a period of about thirty seconds, State Trooper Lt. Spencer and I couldn't hear ourselves think. But as soon as the three bikers exited the lot and took off down the long gravel drive, the tall trees muted the sound of the motorcycles.

"Not a big fan of Harleys," Lt. Spencer said. "Nor the bikers who ride them."

"Can't say I blame you, Lieutenant," I said. "Come

on inside. Mrs. Torchi is using the phone right now. As you might imagine, she's pretty upset. But she's rallied the strength to begin making arrangements for her husband's funeral."

"I understand," he said. "Sheriff Woods has filled me in on just about everything. I'm told Mr. Torchi's death was an accident, so I'll just need your statements and I'll be out of your hair."

"Right this way," I said, ever the respectful citizen.

The state trooper took off his Stetson and followed me up the steps onto the porch. Whether he knew it or not, he was about to confront the grieving widow of a very bad man.

I opened the door for him, and we both immediately caught sight of Cora using the landline on the check-in counter. When she saw that a state trooper had just walked in, she didn't register shock but instead, wiped the tears from her eyes. Like I said, either she was genuinely upset with Sonny's passing, or she was as good an actor as they came. She said something into the phone while gesturing to us with her free hand as if to say, hang on one second.

When she hung up the phone, she wiped her eyes again and said, "How can I help you, Officer?"

Lieutenant Spencer approached her, introduced himself, and told her in as few words as possible why he was here.

"I won't be but a minute, Mrs. Torchi," he said. "Naturally, I understand how upset you must be."

She wiped her eyes yet again and came around the desk.

"I just spoke with Sonny's mother," she said. "She's getting on in years, but the news of her son's death will probably kill her."

"No mother should have to bury her child," Spencer said. Then, after a beat, "Is there somewhere we can talk? You and Mr. Kingsley here."

Cora pointed at the empty tavern and the empty tables

inside it.

"Take a seat, please," she said. "I'll put on some coffee. I expect people to start coming around soon. Sonny had a lot of friends in the community. He did a lot for Loon Lake. Or, he wanted to do a lot, anyway."

It was the perfect touch, I thought. Make the state trooper think Sonny was not a mobster bent on stealing Loon Lake right out from under the residents, but instead, a pillar of the community. Unless this trooper was one of the lawmen in Sonny's pocket. But if he wasn't, then it was entirely possible he took Cora's words at face value.

Cora went into the kitchen while Trooper Spencer and I took a seat and sat in silence. Until he broke it by asking if I lived in Loon Lake. I had a choice here. I could either fib and say I was working for Sonny full-time, or I could just come out with the plain truth, Sing Sing warts and all. I decided the best plan was to go with the latter since Woods would have had no choice but to reveal my true past.

"I'm going to be perfectly honest with you, Lieutenant Spencer," I said. "I'm an ex-con."

He seemed suddenly taken aback, like he didn't meet many ex-cons up in the beautiful Adirondack Mountains, even if there were two major maximum security joints located up there. He pulled out his smartphone, pressed a couple of icons, and set it onto the table.

"Mind if I record your statement?" he asked. "If you want to call a lawyer first, that's perfectly fine. This is for records purposes only. For my report. Nothing more."

"It's fine," I said. "I have nothing to hide." It was a lie, of course, but what the hell choice did I have in the matter?

"Your full name?" he asked.

I told him. When he asked me my age, occupation, and address of official residence, I gave those to him, too. I revealed my overseas Army service and made a point of telling him that I was a combat vet. I simply went with the truth. I gave him my home address in Albany, even though

I'd likely never step foot inside the place again. Told him I was a writer who was temporarily working for Sonny Torchi while I got back on my feet now that I had been paroled. Told him I was about to be going through a divorce. All of it, the truth.

He nodded sympathetically.

"I've seen it happen more than once," he said.

"What's that?" I said.

"A man goes to prison for a while, comes back to an empty house." He shook his head, pursed his thick lips. "Women get itchy when they're alone."

I thought about Leslie, saw her pretty face. A pretty face that I both adored and hated at the same time. I saw her, in my mind, fucking the carpenter I paid to install a new bathroom. I saw myself tossing him through the big plate glass window. Saw myself pounding his head on the pavement, saw the blood smearing on the concrete patio, heard the screams of the Lucy's Bar patrons for me to stop. Felt Stan and Theresa pulling me off of him before I did end up committing murder.

The trooper asked me what I was in for, where I was sent up, and for how long. I told him, gave him the precise dates of my incarceration. He nodded.

"You're lucky," he said. "Most men in your situation would be doing at least ten to twenty. How did you get such a lenient sentence?"

"Guy I beat up didn't want to press charges since he felt bad about screwing around with my wife behind my back. DA saw it otherwise, of course. This is New York State, after all, where the bad guy is usually considered the good guy. So, I did twenty months of a three-year aggrivated assault sentence."

"I see," he said, pursing those lips again. "It was your first and only violation, I'm assuming?"

"Never so much as a parking ticket."

He scrunched his brow.

"Okay," I said, "I'm lying about that. But you get my point."

"I do, Mr. Kingsley." He reached into his chest pocket, pulled out a small notebook and a pen. He handed them to me. "If you would be so kind as to write down the name and phone number of your parole officer, I would be much obliged."

Naturally, I did it for him. I handed it back to him.

"Sheriff Woods over at Loon Lake township has been in contact with my parole officer as well," I added.

"Okay, good," he said. "Sounds like you're handling everything the right way and covering your bases."

Cora came back in then with three cups of coffee set on a round tray which she placed on the table. There was also some sugar, milk, and spoons set on the tray. She passed around the coffees and sat back down. She stared into her coffee, looking defeated and drained.

Wrapping her hands around her coffee cup, she raised her head.

"So, how can I help you, Lieutenant?" she asked.

He gave her the same song and dance about recording the conversation, which she agreed to. He then asked her the last time she saw her husband alive. She exhaled a heavy breath and cleared her throat.

"Last night, I suppose," she said. "When he went to bed. I kissed him goodnight. We both fell asleep, and he got up before dawn to clear the trails along with Mr. Kingsley here."

The trooper took a careful sip of his black coffee and set the cup back down.

"So then, Mr. Kingsley," he said, "it stands to reason that if you were with Mr. Torchi when he suffered his accident, you were the last one to see him alive."

"Technically speaking, the hospital crew who worked on him were the last ones to see him alive, Lieutenant."

He nodded.

"Allow me to rephrase," he said. "You were with him when he had his accident. Maybe you can recall for me what happened exactly."

This was where I had to be careful. I needed to be crystal clear in my explanation, but at the same time, I had to keep it short, sweet, and simple as all hell. Just in case he asked me to repeat it again and again, which he was sure to do. Maybe not today, but if he suspected something was screwy with my testimony, he would call me back in for repeated interviews. Which meant I'd better create a story that was not only simple but also one that I could repeat over and over again without changing it.

"I'd be happy to tell you," I said. Then, my eyes on Cora, "You sure you want to hear this, Mrs. Torchi? It's not very pretty."

"It's okay," she said. "I want to know, too. No, that's not right. I need to know."

I drank some coffee, wishing to God there was a double shot of whiskey in it, and then I told him the story. About how we started clearing the Loon Lake Trail at dawn. About how it was hard, sweaty work. About how the chainsaw was an old piece of shit. How unsafe it was. How it ran out of gas and oil after about a half mile of clearing. Since I was the one carrying the gas and oil cans, Mr. Torchi instructed me to fill the chainsaw up with both while he took a rest, which I proceeded to do.

Then, I told him I must have accidentally got some oil on the chainsaw's trigger because when he started it up, the saw slipped from his hand and cut into his leg. The cut was so deep it must have cut his femoral artery. He was bleeding so bad, I applied a tourniquet. Knowing he couldn't possibly walk, and that I couldn't possibly carry him, I did the only sensible thing. I went for help.

The Lieutenant nodded while Cora started crying again. If I had to guess, he was buying my story. If I had to guess something else, he was one of the good cops. Not one of the cops who didn't do anything about the Loon Lake family that got burned to death.

He stood.

"This has been a very hard day for you both," he said, picking up his phone, and stashing it in the chest pocket on his gray uniform shirt. "That's all I'll need for now. Naturally, I'll check in with the sheriff to see if your story corroborates with his."

"Why wouldn't it?" I said.

"Just standard operating procedure in a matter such as this one."

He thanked Cora for the coffee and started for the door.

But then he turned at the last second.

"Oh, and I'll need the chainsaw," he said. "We'll need to do a forensics examination on it to go along with the autopsy."

His words felt like a punch to the stomach. The chainsaw. It never dawned on me that the cops would want to confiscate it.

"I have to be honest," I said. "I think it's still on the trail where we left it."

"Not a problem," he said. "In fact, soon as I leave here, I'm going to send in a forensics team from out of Plattsburgh to photograph the scene of the accident."

My mouth went dry. I tried to swallow but I couldn't.

"Why would you need forensics for an accident?" I asked, knowing that if I pressed too hard, he might become suspicious. Or maybe he already was suspicious, and that was the reason for the forensics team in the first place.

"Again," he said, "SOP, Mr. Kingsley. State troopers like to be thorough in our investigations."

"I get it," I said.

Now I really needed a drink.

"One last question, Mrs. Torchi," the lieutenant went on. "Did your husband happen to have any life insurance?"

Cora shook her head.

"He had a small policy for the business," she said.

190

The Caretaker's Wife

"But otherwise, his family has money. He never felt the need to buy a personal policy."

The lieutenant smiled, but it wasn't a very nice smile.

"Who really thinks they're going to die?" he said.

Turning, he opened the door and left the tavern.

Vincent Zandri

20

As soon as I heard his car door shut and his engine fire up, I got up, made my way around the bar and poured myself a shot of whiskey. A generous shot.

"He knows," I said, slamming down the shot, pouring another. "He fucking knows."

"Knows what, Kingsley?" Cora said. "He thinks it was an accident and now he's just double checking that it was nothing more. It's his job to be thorough."

"I still don't like it," I said. "My gut doesn't like it. My built-in shit detector doesn't like it. If what Woods tells me is right and most of the troopers around here are corrupt, then isn't it my dumb luck that the one honest cop latches on to me? I should have taken care of the damned chainsaw when I had the chance."

"And what exactly were you going to do with it? Toss it in the lake?"

She had a point. If I'd tossed the saw away, it just would have made me look guilty. Still, for a quick minute, I thought about heading back out on the trail and stealing the chainsaw. But that would be too obvious. Maybe I could set it on fire, or yank off the chain and toss that in lake. But I knew it was all too late for that. The state cops would know that the saw had been tampered with after the fact. It was exactly the kind of thing Spencer's forensics team would be looking for. Something that would prove Sonny's accident wasn't an accident at all, but instead a murder.

Cora got up, came around the bar. She placed a fresh glass onto the bar, poured herself a small shot.

"So, how did you do it?" she asked.

"You really want to know?" I said.

"Yes, Kingsley. Like I said before, I want to know."

I drank what was left in my glass, and I told her exactly how it happened. I even added the part about the black bear dragging him further into the woods after he'd bled out. How the sheriff shot the bear with his pistol. I told her I couldn't make this stuff up even if I were writing a novel.

"Sweet Jesus," she said. "I'm not sure even a man as bad as Sonny deserved to die like that."

"The point is, he's dead, and now we have each other. It's what we wanted, right?"

She drank her drink, slapped the empty glass on the bar.

"Then why does it feel so fucking bad?" she said.

For a minute we didn't say a word. But the silence was quickly broken with the sound of another vehicle pulling up outside. We both came back around the bar and went to the window. It was Sheriff Woods. He wasn't here for a social call or to offer up his condolences to Cora, that much was for sure. He got out of the prowler and approached the tavern, his scruffy face tight as a tick. I'd already opened the door for him before he reached it.

"Cora," he said, touching the brim of his cowboy hat.

"Sheriff," she said.

He turned to me. "The state police been to see you?" he asked.

"Just left," I said. "I'm surprised you didn't run into him on your way in here. Black guy by the name of Spencer."

"He spoke with me earlier. Maybe he didn't say anything about it, but I get the feeling he's got his doubts about Sonny's situation being an accident."

Despite the calming effects of the whiskey, my stomach cramped up and my temples started to pound like two tympani inside my brain.

I said, "Spenser said he's sending out a forensics team to examine the site where the accident happened. He also wants the chainsaw."

Cora took a step forward.

"We all know that Sonny's death was no accident," she said. "If Spencer is a good trooper surrounded by bad troopers, he'll want to get to the bottom of what happened."

Her words were like a blow to the gut. Because what she was saying was this: it was only a matter of time until Spencer found out the truth.

"I was thinking about going back into the woods to retrieve the chainsaw," I said.

"Don't," Woods said. "It's too late for that, and the staties will know you tampered with it and they'll use it against you."

"That's what I said," Cora added. "It would only make matters worse."

"Besides," the sheriff went on, "we've got bigger problems to deal with." He focused on Cora. "Cora, I assume you notified Sonny's family about what happened this morning?"

"I told his mother," she said.

"Listen," Woods went on. "Big Billy has already been 'round to see me. He's convinced Sonny was assassinated. If he's convinced of that, then the entire Torchi family will be convinced of that, never mind the state cops."

"So, what are you saying?" Cora said.

"What I'm saying is the Torchi crime family wants war, not later but now."

I swallowed something bitter while the timpani inside my head got louder.

"They're on their way?" I said. "You're sure about that?"

"That meeting we called for later on at Bunny's?" the sheriff said. "It's been moved up to now."

"What about the state troopers coming here with their forensics team?"

"Forget about them," Woods said. "Right now, we need a plan to protect this town from the inevitable."

"What's the inevitable?" I said.

"War, Kingsley," he said. "Our all-out war against the mob."

Cora and I followed Woods back into town. We parked beside him in Bunny's parking lot. I had to be honest. As much as I loved Cora...as much as I had been willing to do anything for her...I was beginning to feel something welling up inside of me. And it wasn't good. It was the need to get the hell out of town. I had a state trooper on my ass, and now I found myself having to help a powerless sheriff defend his own town from a bunch of very pissed off gangsters who were sure to show up with some heavy weaponry.

Was it worth the one-hundred grand I'd been promised? What if, in the end, I helped Woods hold back the Torchi crime syndicate and I was arrested for Sonny's murder anyway? I would be kicking myself for not having taken advantage of a head start to the Canadian border while I had the chance.

But then again, maybe I was just panicking. I wasn't one for panicking. Panic was another one of those things that would get you killed on the battlefield and in the joint. What was the old saying the Brits liked so much? Keep calm and carry on. I was a part of this thing now. There was no getting away from that. When I personally killed Sonny Torchi, I had done this crummy little nowhere town a service. But at the same time, I'd placed a curse on them. If what Sheriff Woods said was true, in only a matter of hours they were gonna get hit, and they were gonna get hit hard, and only a handful of us could stop them.

It was suddenly dawning on me that we'd be lucky to escape with our lives.

We followed the sheriff into the bar. Maybe a couple dozen people were present. Men mostly, but a few women mixed in. Some of them were seated at the bar, drinking beers from mugs or from out of the bottles. Sheriff Woods took up a position over at the pool table, only he wasn't about to play pool. He pulled a document from out of his chest pocket, unfolded it, and laid it out on the table. It was a map of the town.

Bunny stood behind the bar along with Kate. Something that surprised me. This morning, I'd assumed Kate was innocent of all this mob and gangster business. But it turned out she was not only interested in saving lives, she was just as interested in saving her town. She wouldn't be here otherwise.

"Kingsley," Sheriff Woods said, "I'll ask you to lock the door and put the closed for business sign out."

Nodding, I turned and flipped the sign that hung from a small nail on the front door from open to closed. Then I closed the door and locked it.

The sheriff asked for quiet. The steady banter immediately stopped. It told me these townspeople still respected Sheriff Woods regardless of how powerless he'd become since the Torchis moved in.

"First off, everyone," he said, "this man to my right is Johnathan Kingsley. Some of you might know of him as JA Kingsley, the author. He's recently come to our community to stay at Loon Lake Inn to write a new book. In the process, he went to work for Sonny Torchi. Upon learning what Torchi and his men were doing to our community, he did something that took a lot of guts. More guts than any of us in this room possess, me included. He neutralized Mr. Torchi and did so with absolute prejudice, and for that we thank him."

The whole room erupted in applause, sending a cold chill up and down my backbone. Here I was standing beside Cora, Sonny's wife, and they were cheering me on for killing her husband. It was perhaps the strangest display I'd ever encountered in my life. Stranger than anything I'd ever written, stranger than anything I'd ever read or watched on the TV, stranger than anything I'd seen or been a part of in prison, stranger than anything on the battlefields of Iraq.

"Naturally," Woods went on, "our discussion in this bar stays in this bar, which is why only a chosen few have been invited to hear what I'm about to say. I trust you all, and I feel quite certain you trust me in return. As we all know, the Torchi family is intent on taking over our small town and turning it into one big casino and illicit drug den. And for this, they have attempted to buy us out for pennies on the dollar. Pathetic offers almost all of us have refused. But in the face of that refusal has come harassment, the demand of illegal cash kickbacks, and even the murder of an entire family—the Kennedys, who died in a tragic house fire not long ago. While that fire was determined to be an accident, witnesses said that Sonny Torchi and his men were witnessed as having been on the scene the night the fire started. A fact that the state police chose to conveniently ignore, especially considering four unidentified troopers also witnessed the quadruple homicide. Two children and two adults died in that fire, and it proved the lengths Torchi was willing to go to, to get what he wanted. And we also know that he has the manpower behind him to cause a lot of hurt to our surviving residents if we don't eventually give his family what they want.

"But all that has changed with the arrival of Mr. Kingsley, who personally managed to enact the ultimate revenge on Torchi. However, in doing so, I'm certain what we are about to face, in a matter of hours I might add, is a gangland assault on our town by the Torchi crime family. What this means is we are not only going to have to defend ourselves, we are going to be expected to fight for every square inch of precious soil under our feet so that once and for all, the Torchi family will leave us alone, leave us in peace. Mr. Kingsley is not only a man of letters, he is a man who knows how to fight and how to survive. He was decorated for bravery in Iraq when his outfit almost singlehandedly took Fallujah in what was arguably the bloodiest battle of the war. He also spent nearly two full years inside a maximum security prison for a crime he was perfectly justified in committing, and he survived. Like I said, he's not only taken care of Sonny Torchi, he's agreed to assist us in our dangerous mission."

They were all looking at me stone-faced, except for Bunny, who raised her fist in the air and shouted, "You go, Mr. Kingsley! You've got some steel balls."

Some of the bar cracked up at that, but the atmosphere quickly turned serious again. One man at the bar raised his hand and said he had a question.

"Why don't we try to approach the state police, Sheriff?" he said. "It's the right and legal thing to do."

Sheriff Woods shook his head.

"Now, Ben," he said, "with all due respect, we've tried that approach in the past when the Kennedys were killed and the state police, in the face of overwhelming evidence to the contrary, called it an accident. Remember the four unidentified troopers I just spoke about? Their presence at the murder scene told me that the Torchis had gotten to them. That they were being paid off in order to tip the scales of justice in their favor." He set his right hand on his gun, almost like he was getting ready to draw it. "And even if we did go to the police, they would insist we stand down and do things according to the letter of the law. In other words, they would disarm us and leave us vulnerable to the attack that is sure to come."

Ben bit down on his lip, nodded, and drank some beer. In my gut, I knew that Woods was absolutely right. If the police were in cahoots with the Torchi family, then the town was on its own. It also meant that I could very well find myself on the losing end of the Sonny Torchi accident investigation. But that would have to wait for a while.

"Now," Woods went on, "I'm going to officially deputize Mr. Kingsley here and a few more of you. When that's done, we're going to get down to making a plan to defend our town against the invaders. Sound good, everyone? Are we all on the same page?"

"Damn straight, Sheriff," Bunny said. "I'll be the first to volunteer to be deputized."

Woods smiled, said, "Well then, come on over here, Bunny, and grab your star."

Bunny came around the bar and went to the pool table. Woods reached into his work shirt pocket, pulled out a gold star, and pinned it to Bunny's black, sleeveless CBGB t-shirt. The look on her face told me this was indeed a proud moment for her.

"Mr. Kingsley," he said, "you're next."

I got my badge, so did Cora and Kate, and so did three other men. We then gathered around the map. Woods pointed at the one road that led into the town from the south. Loon Lake Road.

"They're sure to come via this route, Kingsley," he said. "What do you suggest we do when they arrive?"

I stared at the map and the different properties that flanked it. Single and two-storied structures mostly. It didn't take a lot of thought on how to handle what would essentially constitute an ambush. We'd set up plenty of them in Iraq and especially Fallujah when we allowed the bandits to enter a roadway while we quietly waited for the right moment to spring our trap on them. It was a classic flanking counter-attack measure, and when enacted with some skill and surprise, it almost always worked.

I glanced at Cora. She looked into my eyes and smiled. It had been a rough day, to say the least, and things were only going to get rougher over the next twenty-four hours. I cleared my throat.

"First, let me say this," I said. "I'm not here to save your town. Fact is, just a few days ago, I was still sleeping behind iron bars inside Sing Sing. If someone told me then that I'd be defending a town that was about to be attacked by a crime syndicate, I would have told them to take another sip. But here I am. What I do, and what I have done, I don't do for Loon Lake. I do it for Cora. And that's all."

It's not one of my favorite clichés, but I'm going to say it anyway. You could have heard a pin drop inside the bar. They were all looking at me like I was their heaven-sent savior, and I was nothing of the sort. I was just a guy who had fallen in love with a mobster's wife—the caretaker's wife. But then, I was also a guy who knew how to kill.

"We allow them to enter the town, Sheriff," I said after a time. "In fact, when they get here, there will appear to be no one on the street. Loon Lake will seem to be deserted. Like a ghost town. The men and women they send will be the toughest of the tough. They will be highly trained cold-blooded killers. But when they ride into this town and discover that it's been emptied, it won't sit right with them. It will send cold chills up and down their backbones. And..." I trailed off.

"And what?" Sheriff Woods said.

"And then we kill them," I said. "Every last one of them. One by one. Methodically. Without hesitation. Without humanity. Without remorse. Without God. We do everything in our power to make the hunters know they are now the hunted." Inhaling and exhaling a deep breath, I then said, "What I'm trying to tell you is that they must be convinced they've just stepped through the gates of hell."

21

It was far too late in the day for the Torchi family to enact their revenge. But my gut told me they would be here prior to the dawn. They would use the sleepy time just minutes before the sunrise to launch their attack—what they no doubt considered a surprise attack.

But we'd be ready for them.

For the next three or four hours we gathered as many hunting rifles as we could. 30.30s, AR15s, shotguns, pistols, and even a bow and arrow that Kate preferred to hunt with. I positioned several men on top of the jail/sheriff's office and several more directly across the street on top of Bunny's Place. I was careful to warn them not to get caught up on one another's crossfire, but instead to fire at the invaders from a thirty-five-degree angle as the bastards made their way towards them. When the surviving gangsters passed by, they were to shift themselves and shoot them from behind. That is, shoot them in the back.

Kate and Bunny would be positioned at the entrance

to the town. They, too, would shoot the bandits in the back as they went by. I told them to take every opportunity to shoot them in the back since the bandits wouldn't hesitate to do the same.

The sheriff and I would be the last line of defense on top of the insurance building across from the sheriff's office. Or, that's the way I planned it anyway. But when Cora insisted she join the sheriff and me at what she described as The Alamo, I couldn't possibly refuse her.

While we stood inside the sheriff's office, she took hold of one of the 9mm semiautomatics, released the magazine, checked the load, then slapped the mag back home while engaging the safety. Stuffing the barrel of the pistol into her leather belt, she helped herself to two additional magazines which she stored in her back pocket. I was a little shocked that Cora knew her way around a gun. But then, she was a former New York City cop, so why should it have surprised me in the least? Making her way to the wall-mounted rifle rack, she grabbed hold of one of the AR15s.

"Magazines, Sheriff?" she asked.

Woods went to his desk, opened the top drawer, and pulled out a key ring. Making his way to the gun safe set beside the gun rack, he slipped a special key into the safe's slot, and then entered a set of four numbers into the safe's electronic locking system. The heavy metal door opened automatically. He reached inside and came back out with several thirty-round magazines.

Handing two to Cora he said, "These are illegal in New York State since our governor reduced the magazine capacity to just seven rounds. But these little babies hold thirty rounds a piece, two-two-three subsonic ammo, so look for big wounds. I've got plenty of them, and they are all loaded."

"Looks like you're ready for the zombie apocalypse, Sheriff," I said.

"No," he said, reaching back into the safe and

pulling out more mags. "I've been preparing for the inevitable showdown with the Torchis for nearly two years now. I upped my preparations after he burned the Kennedys in their own home and the state police refused to do anything about it." He set at least two dozen magazines onto his desk. "The weapons you see here are just a part of my little personal arsenal."

Stepping into the center of the office, he took a knee and pulled back the throw rug, revealing a trap door in the floor. Pulling open the door, he reached down inside and flicked on a light switch.

"Anyone care to follow me down into my secret bunker of tough love?"

Without waiting for an answer, he began descending a metal ladder. Cora didn't hesitate to follow. Neither did I. Standing at the foot of the ladder, I couldn't believe my eyes. It was a small concrete room, not much bigger than a small bedroom. But this place was a far cry from a peaceful night's sleep. Every inch of wall space was covered in weaponry of one kind or another. And I'm not talking garden variety pistols and rifles. Being an ex-Army Ranger, I recognized three grenade launchers which could be mounted to the AR15s. There was one SAM, along with six or so landmines. There was even a .30 caliber tripod mounted machine gun. But what surprised me the most was the flamethrower. If I had to guess, it dated back to the Vietnam War.

"Where'd you get this stuff, Sheriff?" I asked. "It must have cost you a fortune."

"You'd be surprised what you can buy off the dark web," he said. "I had the opportunity to buy a leftover Sherman Tank along with a dozen live cannon shells. I would have too, if it wouldn't be so difficult to conceal."

I glanced at Cora. I got the feeling that she, too, was amazed at the arsenal.

We proceeded to carry most of the special weapons cache upstairs, including the land mines and the .30 cal. By now, it was going on one in the morning, and we figured that a few hours' sleep would be crucial if we were planning on being prepared for the battle that was sure to begin at first light.

"Tell you what," Woods said. "There's a cozy jail cell in back. You two are welcome to use that. No way I'm sleeping tonight. I'll take watch and set the mines while you get some rest."

I thanked the sheriff and then took hold of Cora's hand and led her to jail.

Like the sheriff indicated, the cell was narrow and cramped, but the bunk, besides being so small it hardly fit one person, wasn't as uncomfortable as the hard-as-a-rock bunk I'd been sleeping on at Sing Sing. But I wasn't interested in comfort at that point. I also wasn't interested in sleep. I wanted something else entirely. As soon as I knew that Sheriff Woods had left the building, leaving Cora and me alone, I grabbed hold of her arms and pulled her into me. Our mouths locked and we proceeded to pull one another's clothes off.

She sat on the cot, unbuckled my belt, and unbuttoned my pants. She pulled me out and took me into her mouth, pumping me hard.

I was so rock hard I thought I might explode in a matter of seconds. But I held back and dropped to my knees. I pulled her jeans and panties down, spread her legs, and went at her with my mouth. I worked her hot wetness with my tongue and lips, and I listened to her moaning until the moaning became shouting.

"Don't stop, Kingsley!" she screamed. "Please don't stop!"

When she came, it was like a gusher. Standing, I rolled her over and entered her from behind. It was somewhat awkward because she had to shift her body in a way that prevented her from banging her head against the concrete block wall. But that didn't matter a whole lot because it took me less than a minute to come to that place where I could no longer hold it all in. When I exploded inside her, I filled her with everything I had to give and then some.

We held each other for a time on that cramped cot as the night wore on. The only light in the cell came from a street lamp outside. It bled into the space through a small barred window located at the very top of the far wall. When Cora rolled over and stared up at the ceiling, I knew she had something on her mind besides the pending battle with her late husband's crime family. I couldn't imagine anything heavier than that, but whatever it was, it was causing her real pain.

"They screamed as they burned," she said, somewhat under her breath.

I knew immediately what she was talking about. The Kennedy family. In my mind, I pictured the burned out shell of a house that was still somehow standing in the center of town.

"Sheriff Woods wasn't lying when he said Sonny and his men were there when the family burned to death. Those two kids and their parents."

"Sonny's men," I said. "As in Big Billy and his two hangers-on."

"Meaning Big Billy and some state troopers," she said. "We don't know who exactly, but they were there."

"Why did he do it, Cora?" I asked. "Why would a man even as rotten as Sonny do something so horrible to an innocent family?"

"He wanted to set an example, and he wanted to scare the living daylights out of the entire town, including the sheriff. And he succeeded."

"And that's when the Torchis paid off the state cops." It was a question.

She nodded, then inhaled and exhaled.

"Sonny stood inside the kitchen, his gun in his hand. Big Billy bound the kids and the family to their chairs at the kitchen table. They used duct tape. They purposely didn't gag them because Sonny said he wanted the entire town to hear their screams when they started to burn. He used gasoline so that it would burn fast after the flash. So that the family wouldn't die from smoke inhalation but instead from the flames roasting their flesh." Tears fell from her eyes. "I overhead Billy brag that as the family burned and screamed, he and Sonny just laughed like it was the funniest thing they'd ever seen. They'd even taken selfies of the scene, but I've never seen them. I guess I never wanted to see them. But I vowed then that I would find a way to kill Sonny someday. As soon as the opportunity presented itself, I would find a way to send him to hell. When you came into my life, it was like you had been purposely sent here by some higher God. If not for you, Sonny would still be alive."

"But now we have his family to deal with," I said, my eyes glued to the white light outside the small window.

"We're going to beat them back, Kingsley," she said. "We're going to beat them back, and we're going to kill every last one of them and send them to hell to be with Sonny." She rolled over, turned to me, and grabbed hold of my hand. "Promise me we'll kill them all, Kingsley. Promise me."

I felt my heart pounding inside my ribcage and the drums beating in my head. It was a surreal moment, but it was also a time of reckoning, both for Cora and the town of Loon Lake.

"I promise," I said.

I closed my eyes and soon, I was asleep.

I see them coming from the roof of the concrete building. Men with thick black beards and black scarves wrapped around their heads. Their lead vehicle is a pickup truck with a .50 cal. machine gun mounted to the back. There must be hundreds of them, all packed into pickups armed with tripod-mounted machine guns. I raise my hand. It's the signal for my men to hold their fire.

But when I drop it, we all open up on the enemy,

cutting them to ribbons. Some of the bandits manage to escape the gauntlet. A dozen enter into the building, climb up onto the roof. They begin to mow down our outflanked squad from behind.

I turn to see a bandit staring me in the face. He must be out of ammo because he wants to dance hand-to-hand. We grapple and drop to the roof floor. Our faces are so close, I can smell his sour breath, feel the sweat pouring off his brow. The bandit manages to steal my fighting knife. We fight for control of it. The blade cuts my chest, opens it up. But I'm not in pain. Instead, I am consumed by rage. I overpower the bandit, steal back the knife, and slice his neck so deep the blade connects with the spinal column...

...I find myself surrounded in the prison shower. Six Aryans, heads shaved, muscles bulging out of green prison-issue t-shirts. They've caught me by complete surprise while I'm at my most vulnerable. Naked and showering. They take turns whipping me, sharp metal shavings cutting into the skin on my back, arms, and chest. I drop to the tiled floor. The pain is so severe, so electric, I can't move, can't scream, can't breathe. I watch my own blood circle the drain...

I woke with a start, Cora still asleep beside me. I glanced at my wristwatch. Three a.m. In just a couple hours, the Torchi family, along with Big Billy and his two black leather-wearing goons, would enter the town with the intent to destroy it and everyone in it. The state police would not be there to help. Neither would the Army, nor even God himself. This was more than a battle for survival. It wasn't a battle between good versus bad. More like bad versus evil.

We had guns and assorted weapons and the element of surprise on our side. But knowing how bad Torchi's army would be...how highly trained...we needed something more to combat them with. Something that would let them know without any question whatsoever the townspeople of Loon Lake were no pushovers. In fact, a few of us might even have a few screws loose. What I had in mind would shake the gangsters to their very core. It wouldn't hurt them physically or neutralize them in any way, but believe me when I say, it would mess them up. Or should I say, mess up their brains. What I was about to engage in was psychological warfare.

I slipped off the cot and grabbed my Jeep keys. In the sheriff's office where the weaponry was laid out on the tables and the desk, I grabbed hold of a Colt .45, made sure it was fully loaded, and stuffed the barrel into my pant waist. It was time to pay a quick visit to Crown Point General. More specifically, the medical center morgue.

22

By the time I returned, it was going on five in the morning, and the dawn wasn't far off. The sheriff was standing outside the jail, his AR15 gripped in his hands. Cora was standing beside him. She was also holding an AR15.

"Thought you left us," Woods said.

"Not for good," I said. "I needed to grab something from the hospital. I'm going to need a couple of the men to string it up for us?"

The sheriff approached the Jeep and glanced in back. "Jesus Christ," he said. "How'd you get away with it?"

"I just walked into the morgue and showed the night watchman my badge. He helped me find the drawer in the cooler. Together, we zipped him up in a bag. I signed a couple of forms, and I walked out with him."

"Just like that," the sheriff said.

"Well, that last bit is sort of an exaggeration," I said. "Sonny's deadweight is still no picnic, so the night watchman helped me load him into the Jeep."

"Still don't believe you," the sheriff said.

I reached around, pulled out the .45 I'd taken earlier. "This helped," I said.

"Now I see the light," Woods said with a shake of his head.

Cora started for the Jeep, but I stopped her.

"Don't, Cora," I insisted. "It's not something you need to see right now."

She stopped and turned away. Sheriff Woods pulled his walkie talkie from his belt.

"Ben, come in. Over," he said into the device.

"What is it, Sheriff? Over."

"Need you and two more men to meet me at the jail. Over."

"Copy that, Sheriff. Out."

"So, what did you have in mind, Kingsley?" Woods asked.

I told him my plan. Told him I'd seen this kind of thing happen on the battlefield. He nodded, then shook his head. He was unnerved by the idea, that much was certain. But he knew how effective the plan could be in putting some serious ass fright into the Torchi gangsters.

"You have my blessing," he said after a time.

A couple of minutes later, Ben and two other men approached the Jeep. They saw the body bag in back. When Ben unzipped the bag, revealing the dead face, there was little doubt they were dealing with something unusual. Something very dark. I told them my plan, and, to my surprise, they were rather pleased with it.

"Don't forget the gasoline," I said. "And make sure Kate is able to use one of her arrows as a fire starter. Wait for my signal."

They nodded in agreement. Then they took the body with them, carrying it up the road to the start of town. I turned to the sheriff.

"It will be first light in a half hour," I said. "Everyone

in position."

"Everyone except us," he said. "You'd better weapon up, Kingsley. You're going to need more than that .45"

"Got any coffee going?"

"It's fresh and hot," he smiled. "Donuts too."

"Breakfast of champions and warriors," I said.

I headed inside the sheriff's office and poured myself a black coffee. While I was drinking it, I prepped myself for war. I proffered one of the sheriff's tactical vests which were hanging on the wall and loaded it with six thirty-round magazines.

I attached one of the grenade launchers to the AR15's rack-mount system and stuffed four grenades in the upper vest pockets.

I shifted the Colt .45 from my pant waist to a plastic holster that clipped onto my belt and added three more nine-round magazines to the vest load. On the opposite hip, I strapped on a fighting knife. I looked around for a helmet, but the sheriff didn't seem to have one, which struck me as odd. Or maybe there were none left. He did have a Loon Lake law enforcement baseball cap, which I put on. It would at least help with reducing the glare that was sure to come with the rising sun. My aviator sunglasses would help, too, since they were Polaroids. Last, but not at all least, I confiscated one of the extra pairs of tactical gloves. Take it from one who knew, you could put a lot of rounds through an AR15, but that barrel still got hot, so the gloves would be a necessity if the shooting lasted a long time, which it was bound to do.

I was just finishing up testing my walkie talkie when Woods came back in along with Cora. They, too, were geared up for war. He pulled out the city map he'd used at Bunny's bar, unfolded it, and laid it on the desk.

"Here, here, and here," he said, pointing at the very center of town with an extended index finger. "These are the locations of the six mines. I set them in pairs just in case the bandits decide to drive on both sides of the street. The first ones don't get them, they're bound to run over the second or third pairs."

"That alone could cripple them," Cora added, her AR15 cradled in her arms.

Sheriff Woods cocked his head, pursed his lips. "Maybe," he said. "My guess is their vehicles will be armored, so landmines might actually be ineffective. We won't know until they trigger them."

I stared at the map.

"My little grisly surprise for them will happen here," I said, pointing to the town entry not far from the funeral parlor. "Right at the start of the town."

"Let's hope it has the psychological effect you're going for," Woods said. "I'm not one for disturbing the dead, even if it's for a good cause."

"Oh, I'm sure Sonny doesn't mind," I said, staring at the floor, as if staring into hell itself. "Do you, Sonny? Can you hear me? Or is the devil keeping you busy?"

But as soon as I said it, I saw an American soldier, stripped naked, nailed to a cross in the middle of the road just outside Fallujah. We went on to fight and win the day anyway, but never before had I been so scared. The enemy had gotten inside our heads that day, and that's what I was hoping to do to the Torchi family. Them and Big Billy and his two cohorts. When it came to love and war, there were no rules. There was only winning and losing, and in this case, losing meant sure death.

Then came a voice over the walkie talkies. It was Ben.

"We've spotted four SUVs led by three motorcycles about a half mile out along Loon Lake Road, Sheriff," he said. "Over."

"Copy," Woods said. "Take your places, Ben. This is it. Over."

"Roger that," Ben said. "God speed and out."

The three of us went outside. Cora started for her position across the street in The Alamo—the insurance building where she would head up onto the roof.

"Wait," I said.

She stopped, turned. I pulled her to me, kissed her. "Don't stop shooting until they're all dead," I said. "No prisoners, you got that? No prisoners."

She gazed at me with wide, beautiful but determined eyes. It was like she'd been waiting for this very moment all her life.

Sheriff Woods got behind the wheel of the prowler and backed it into the middle of the road. He killed the ignition and got out but left the door open so that he could use it as a protective barrier. I opened the passenger side door and took up a defensive position behind it. By then we could easily hear the Harleys, telling me Big Billy was riding point, just like we figured he would.

Gazing at the sheriff, I gave him a nod and a thumbs-up.

"Let's do this, Kingsley," he said.

"Ben," I said, into my chest-mounted walkie talkie. "Light up the body."

As the sun came up on the main street of the Loon Lake Township, something very disturbing appeared in the middle of the road at the very entrance to the town. It was the naked, dead corpse of Sonny Torchi, and it was nailed to a homemade cross.

An arrow shot out of the sky. The tip of the arrow was aflame, and when it struck home at the base of the cross, it ignited the entire gasoline-soaked crucifix.

"Great shot, Kate," I said into my walkie talkie.

"I aim to please," she responded, "even if this is one of sickest displays I've ever witnessed."

"It's a necessary evil," I said. Then, "Okay, everyone, you all know what to do. Don't shoot until you can make out their eyes and the first of the mines have detonated. Over and out."

The motorcycles were now in view. Billy was out front

by about twenty feet, his two cohorts behind him. He was holding onto the handlebars with one hand and with the other, he held a mini-M16—the shorter barreled version of the full-sized automatic rifle. He stopped his bike maybe ten feet away from the burning cross. His scream was so loud it rattled my teeth.

Behind him and his two men appeared four black Suburbans with tinted windows. It was Torchi's army. The cross was fully ignited when Billy pulled ahead. But that's when something happened that must have taken Billy by complete surprise. His two Harley riding cohorts wouldn't follow. They were so frightened, I could almost smell it. Sensing they weren't moving ahead, Billy stopped and turned to face them.

"What the hell is the matter with you two?" he barked. "We've got a hunting party to lead."

"I don't like this," one of them yelled. "That's some crazy shit hanging on that cross, Billy."

"And where is everyone?" the other one shouted. "It's like the town is abandoned."

Billy dismounted his motorcycle and gripped his mini-M16 with both hands. He shouldered the weapon and aimed it at his own men.

"Move forward," he barked. "Or die."

But they wouldn't move. That's when Billy fired on his own men, taking them both out with one single, extended rifle burst. Woods and I exchanged glances because we knew exactly what the other was thinking. The first casualties of this war were suffered by the enemy, and the casualties were inflicted upon themselves.

My idea to crucify Sonny's corpse might have been a sick display, just like Kate said. But the terror tactic also worked. Worked like a charm.

Big Billy got back on his bike and slowly made his way along the road while the vehicles followed. He was maybe one-hundred-fifty feet away from where the sheriff and I were positioned when the first of the SUVs ran over a landmine.

The explosion rocked the town. That was when every deputy and townsperson with a gun opened up on the four Suburbans. Six men poured out of the vehicle that had taken the blast. One of them was on fire. I planted a bead on the burning man and fired. The headshot dropped him on the spot. The others began returning the crossfire that was coming from the roof of Bunny's Place and on top of the jail. Two of our men immediately went down, falling from the roof. But two of their men also dropped in the road.

Sheriff Woods shifted to the .30 cal. and began pouring lead into the surviving Suburbans. He also took out a number of bandits at the same time. He fired until one full belt was gone, and then he transitioned back to his AR15.

I tried to find Big Billy, but he had disappeared. No doubt, he ran for cover as soon as the first Suburban detonated the mine. His Harley was sitting in the middle of the road. I wasn't entirely sure what made me do it, but I loaded the grenade launcher with one of my four grenades, took aim, and blew the bike to Kingdom Come. The smile on my face went from ear to ear.

I did, however, glance up at the roof of The Alamo. Cora had her AR15 shouldered, and she was firing down on the bandits who'd just escaped the burning Suburban. Not a single one of them was left standing after she was through with them. Turns out, the love of my life was a crack shot.

The second Suburban tried to get around the first, now disabled, Suburban. The men inside it weren't foolish enough to get out. They were firing from the open windows. Woods was firing directly into the vehicle's windshield. But the rounds were bouncing off.

"Fucking bulletproof glass!" he shouted while dropping his empty magazine and replacing it with a full one.

"Whad'ya expect?" I shouted. "These bastards know what they're doing!"

When the second Suburban detonated another landmine, it took even me by surprise. One by one the unhurt bandits escaped the burning SUV. This time, however, instead of leaving themselves exposed to the rooftop fire, they took up defensive positions behind the two unharmed vehicles. The shots from their automatic weapons were deadly accurate. Two more of our men had been gunned down. But when I saw an arrow strike one of the bandits square in the chest, I knew Kate was still alive and still fighting.

I turned to make a quick check on Cora on the roof of The Alamo. She was firing steadily at the bandits. But they were too well dug in now. It was a stalemate. That's when I decided to make my way around the prowler to the sheriff.

"We gotta outflank those vehicles or sooner than later they're gonna get the jump on us," I said.

"Grenades," he said. "You go right, and I'll go left, while Cora shoots down the middle."

"Copy that," I said.

Turning, I sprinted for the sherriff's office. I made my way inside, ran to the back where the jail was located, and exited the building by way of the emergency exit. Hooking a left, I sprinted along the backs of the commercial buildings that lined the main street, until I was parallel with the two surviving Suburbans.

"I'm in place, Sheriff Woods. Over," I spoke into my walkie talkie.

"Copy that," he said. "Me too. Fire at will. Over."

Loading my grenade launcher, I took aim at the vehicle closest to me. I fired. The explosion lifted the vehicle off the ground and sent it crashing back down. The bandits turned to me, started firing at my position. I mowed them down as quickly as the rounds could leave my barrel. And when I ran out of ammo, I dropped the magazine, and without shifting my aim, loaded a fresh one into the rifle, and resumed firing.

When the last remaining Suburban blew sky high,

The Caretaker's Wife

I knew then that we firmly had the upper hand. That's when I made out the chop-chop sound of rotors and, looking up, I caught sight of the blue and yellow chopper heading directly for our positions.

I spotted the rockets' red glare even before I heard their noise. Because, after all, light travels faster than sound. The first rocket blew the grocery store to bits. It also caused the gas pumps to blow. The earth shook, and the sky seemed like it was set on fire. The second rocket took out most of Bunny's bar and, from what I could see, most of the men and women who were defending it. The third rocket took out the hardware store and for certain, Kate. My heart dropped to somewhere around my ankles.

"You bastards!" I screamed at the chopper.

The final rocket took out the sheriff's office. Just like that, the entire town was ablaze in an inferno of fire and black smoke. The fucking state police...they were fighting on the side of the Torchi crime syndicate.

"Everyone who hears this!" I barked into the walkie talkie. "Anyone who is still alive and able to walk. Head to The Alamo now! Over!"

I made my way back the way I came. Only this time, there was no sheriff's office to provide access to the main street. There was only burning rubble which I was forced to go around. When I sprinted my way across the street, I was met with automatic gunfire that ricocheted against the street, sending chunks of macadam up into my face. When I came to the glass insurance office door, I didn't bother to stop to pull the door open. Instead, I lowered my shoulder and plowed right through it, shattering the glass.

Cora had already made her way down from the roof, and she was changing out the magazine on her AR15.

"We're screwed," she said, gritting her teeth. "Fucking state solice...fucking on the take, New York State Police. Could it get any worse? We're all dead, Kingsley. We're all dead."

219

She cocked her weapon, shouldered it, and went to the now demolished front door. She took aim and fired at the enemy out the door opening.

"Here comes Woods," she yelled. "Help me with covering fire."

I went to the door and took a knee. She would aim high, I'd go low. Sheriff Woods was sprinting in our direction while the bandits were firing at him with everything they had. But Cora and I returned their fire and were able to cover the sheriff as he made his way safely inside The Alamo.

"Goddamn," he said, his face ruddy with dirt and sweat, his cowboy hat pulled far down on his forehead. "That chopper is gonna come back, and when it does, there won't be a building left to defend ourselves with in Loon Lake."

That's when I recalled the SAM down inside the sheriff's office bunker.

"What about the SAM?" I said.

He glanced in the direction of his office and the jail behind it. What was left of it, I should say.

"Good chance one of us will get shot trying to get at it," he said. "But it might be worth the risk."

"I'll go," Cora said.

"The hell you will," I said. "I should do it. The state police are already on me about Sonny's death. I have as much of a personal grudge against those bastards as you do."

"We'll cover you," the sheriff said.

My AR15 gripped in both hands, I stood at the open door, and like a sprinter on his mark, I waited for the sheriff's signal.

"Go!" he spat as he and Cora fired out the door.

I sprinted across the street, the bandits' rounds whizzing and buzzing past my head like angry wasps. I fired back at them from the hip, not really hoping to hit anything, just hoping that the gunfire would be enough to make them take cover. It seemed to take me forever to get to the destroyed office. But when I finally made it, I jumped over the rubble and found the door in the floor. I opened it and quickly made my way down the metal ladder.

The SAM was still mounted to the wall. So was the flamethrower. Without thinking about it, I grabbed both. I slung the AR15 around my back and carried the SAM and the flamethrower with me up the ladder and onto the office floor. The bullets were still whizzing past me and ricocheting against the damaged concrete block wall. I knew if one of those bullets found a home in the gasoline-filled flamethrower, it would blow me apart.

Sucking in a breath, I crouched and sprinted my way back to The Alamo, the SAM in one hand and the flamethrower in the other. Only when I made it back inside did I finally release my breath.

"Back up to the roof," I said.

Together, we made our way upstairs and onto the roof. By now the bandits were making their way on foot through the burning remnants of the town. Cora and the sheriff took aim at them and took out two or three more. I was focusing on the sky, my eyes searching for the chopper that was sure to make its return. In the meantime, it looked like an army of black-clad Torchi bandits were making their way toward us. I could make out the sound of men entering The Alamo. Soon, they'd be upstairs and up on the roof.

"Where the hell is that chopper?" I barked.

I hardly got the words out of my mouth when I spotted it. It was assuming the same flight path it had minutes before when it took out most of the town's buildings.

"You know how to work the SAM?" the sheriff shouted.

"You gotta ask?" I said.

"Make the shot count, Kingsley. There's only one round."

"I'll get the bastard," I said. "Don't you worry." Shouldering the SAM, I pulled off the cover, which automatically armed it. Pulling down the trigger guard, I planted a bead on the incoming chopper just as it released a rocket aimed for us, pointblank.

"Incoming!" I screamed as I pressed the SAM trigger.

23

From down on my back, I felt like I was caught up in a dream. I could see the sheriff. He was still firing at the bandits down in the street. I could see Cora down on her knees. She was dazed, that much was obvious. But she was shooting at two bandits who were coming through the door that accessed the roof. Shooting them dead. My head was ringing, my body shaking. When I finally managed to get myself back up onto my feet, I could see that the chopper's missile had struck the exterior wall of The Alamo only six feet below where I was standing. That was bad news. But the good news was that a smoking hunk of blue and yellow metal now resided in the middle of Loon Lake Main Street. It was the downed chopper, its body on fire. By the looks of it, a whole bunch of bandits had been taken out when it crashed.

But the survivors still kept coming at us. The Alamo was severely damaged, and if I didn't know any better, it was on the verge of collapse. As soon as she was finished with clearing out the bandits from the doorway, Cora came to me.

"Oh my God, baby," she said. "Are you hurt bad?"

"A little hard of hearing," I shouted, "but otherwise okay."

Sheriff Woods dropped another empty magazine and slapped a full one home.

"That's my last mag," he said. "The thirty cal is out, too. We gotta end this thing soon, or we're dead people walking."

I spotted the flamethrower then. I picked it up, strapped it on my back.

"How's this work?" I said.

"Let me help," he said, going around my back, turning a couple of valves. Reaching into his pocket, he pulled out a silver Zippo lighter and fired up the gun nozzle. "Just aim and pull the trigger," he said.

Peering down at the dozen or so bandits now making their way around the chopper, I waited until they were within a few feet of the building and then I let them have it. The fire engulfed them, roasted them while they ran around like helpless, screaming blind men. Enough was enough. The fire sucked the life out of their fight. The two or three survivors dropped their weapons, turned tail, and ran in the direction from which they came. Where they thought they were running to was anybody's guess. At that point, it was obvious we had won the battle, but had Loon Lake won the war against the Torchi crime family? Only time would tell. All I knew was I had done my part. I'd done what I'd promised both for Cora and for the sheriff. Now, I had Cora for my own, and soon, I'd be flush with cash.

The flamethrower was still strapped to my back, the smoldering gun nozzle still gripped in my hand when I turned to see him come through the door. It was Big Billy. He was carrying his mini-M16. Before his sudden presence had even fully registered, he triggered a burst at Sheriff Woods that nearly tore the lawman in two at the waist. Cora went after Billy with her bare hands, and the big goon grabbed hold of her hair with one hand while holding the short barreled automatic rifle barrel against her lower spine with the other.

He looked at me, licked his lips, and smiled.

"I don't care that you're an asshole, Kingsley," he said. "I can forgive you for that. Christ, I can even forgive you for killing Sonny, and for killing all my brothers and sisters out there. But what I cannot possibly forgive you for is fucking up my bike. That bike was precious to me. Maybe even as precious as Cora is to you."

"Kill him, Kingsley," Cora shouted. "Burn the motherfucker. Do it. Don't worry about me. Just burn him."

Of course, he had me by the balls, and he knew it. There was no way I was about to sacrifice Cora just to kill the son of a bitch. Instead, I slipped the flamethrower canisters off my back and tossed the whole thing at his feet. For a quick second, he flinched, like maybe he thought the flamethrower might explode. But he quickly assumed his wide, hungry smile once more.

"Now," he said, "the guns, Kingsley. Drop all the guns." I pulled the AR15 off my back, dropped it next to the flame thrower. I was about to pull the .45 from its holster when I noticed the slightest movement coming from Sheriff Woods.

I had no idea how he could still be alive. But I saw him slowly reach for his rifle, saw him place his bloody finger on the trigger. It was important to keep Big Billy's eyes on me. I made sure to slowly draw my .45 so he wouldn't have a clue what the sheriff was up too.

"Just shoot him," Cora insisted. "Just shoot Billy, and this will be over."

Dropping the .45 beside the rifle and the flamethrower, I said, "Bill, look right."

The big man's smile dissolved and he glanced over his right shoulder. That's when the sheriff took a final shot with his dying breath.

Vincent Zandri

24

The round from the AR15 nailed Big Billy in the thigh. But even at that close range, he didn't drop on the spot. He was too big for that. Too strong. He did, however, let go of Cora. She punched him in the wounded thigh and then crawled off to safety. At the same time, I thrust myself at Billy. Wrapping my right hand around his neck, I squeezed as hard as I could. With my left hand, I grabbed hold of my fighting knife. But Billy grabbed hold of the knife at the same time, and he was using all his strength to shove the blade tip into my chest.

Out the corner of my eye, I saw Cora go for my .45. But there was no way she could get a safe shot at Billy with the two of us tangled up like that. If she took a shot, she'd kill us both.

And she must have known it, because she just stood there, the pistol in hand, and her face a mask of pain and anxiety.

"Kill him, Kingsley!" she screamed like a cheerleader. "Kill him!"

But Billy had the upper hand, and I was feeling the electric pain of the blade cutting into the flesh on my chest. I had to do something and do it fast, or this would be over in a matter of seconds. Taking a real chance, I freed up my left hand and began to pound on his thigh wound. That did the trick because he released his hold on the knife and screamed. He also dropped to the floor, taking me with him.

I tried to plunge the knife into his neck then, but he managed to swipe it right out of my hand. He shifted himself onto his knees and, looking into my eyes, he began to choke me. Along with his massive hands crushing my throat, I felt his fury. I felt the hatred. I felt the evil that resided inside his black soul. There was so much evil inside him that he lost all sense of reality. He wanted only to strangle me. That was his singular purpose. His sole purpose. That purpose blinded him. He never saw Cora when she raised the .45, took aim, and fired.

The round hit him in the chest. He released my neck, but he wasn't down yet. He was in such a rage, that he got back up onto his feet. He started to approach Cora, slowly stepping toward her. My head was spinning from lack of oxygen, but I knew I had to gather all of my strength to find a way to put him down for good before he got any closer to her.

She fired again and again, but it wasn't slowing Big Billy down. He was an enraged monster. Only a headshot would finish him off, but she wasn't going for the head. It was then my eyes focused on my AR15 and the flamethrower beside it. Billy was stepping over the flamethrower on his way to Cora when I rolled over, grabbed the rifle, and took aim. Not at Big Billy, but at the flamethrower canisters.

25

The flames immediately engulfed Billy's entire black leather covered body. The fire consumed his legs, arms, torso, plus his head and his face. He screamed a high-pitched wail that came from somewhere deep down inside his gut, and he clawed at his face as it melted off his skull. He dropped to his knees, and he kept on screaming until his mouth and lungs burned away. He fell flat on his face on the rooftop. Cora and I just watched his body burn like a house being consumed by an out of control fire. The Kennedy family house fire came to mind.

"Karma's a bitch, Bill," I said.

When we knew without a doubt he was finally dead, Cora took a step forward, and aiming the .45, emptied the remainder of the nine-round magazine into his charred skull.

"When you get to hell, Billy," she said, "say hello to my husband."

Tears were streaming down her face as Cora made her

way to the open door and, stepping over two or three dead bodies, began her descent back down to the first floor of the insurance building.

Moments later, we stood in the middle of the main street, observing the carnage and the destruction. Dead and severely wounded bodies were everywhere. Some of them had been shot to pieces, some of them burned, others just lying still like they simply lay down and fell into a deep sleep. Buildings were burning or entirely destroyed. So were two of the Suburbans. A crashed state trooper helicopter clogged the middle of the road along with the now shot up Sheriff's prowler. It wasn't like staring at a war zone. It was like staring at the apocalypse.

"What a mess," Cora said after a time.

She then did something I never would have expected. She started to laugh. I could recall some of my men laughing after a particularly hard-fought battle. It seemed like the only way you dealt with all that violent death and destruction was to laugh it off. It was either laugh or go insane. Then, a head emerged from out of what used to be the entry to Bunny's Place. I'll be damned if it wasn't Bunny herself. She'd somehow survived the onslaught. But then, I wasn't the least bit surprised that she had.

I waved her over.

"Come with us, Bunny!" I shouted. "This place is way too hot to stick around!"

"No, thanks," she said. "I'm gonna stay and salvage what I can. I'll catch up with you two later on."

"Be safe, Bun," Cora added.

I took hold of my girl's hand then, and we made our way to my Jeep, which was still parked in front of the sheriff's office. The office itself might have been gone, but the Jeep didn't look a whole lot worse for wear. It had taken a few rounds and some shrapnel damage. The windshield was cracked, but other than that, my Jeep had been spared. I

The Caretaker's Wife

wasn't sure why, but it made me very happy.

I slipped behind the wheel, and Cora got into the passenger seat. Firing it up, I pulled out of the lot and drove in the opposite direction of Loon Lake Inn. I didn't know where we were going, I just took hold of Cora's hand again, held it tightly, and I drove. I drove to nowhere.

Vincent Zandri

26

Sixteen Months Later

News of what was now being called the Battle for Loon Lake spread faster than the fire that consumed Big Billy's body. Cora and I lawyered up with a hotshot attorney from New York City who, in exchange for working pro-bono, was getting himself a ton of air time on all the national news and morning shows. We were interviewed over and over again by members of the state police who apparently weren't on the take, including Lieutenant Spencer who, by now, considered Sonny's untimely death directly related to the war waged in town.

"Of course they're connected," I freely admitted. "It was his family who tried to destroy us."

While the Essex County DA searched for ways to prosecute us on various illegal weapons charges that not only included the use of war-like weaponry such as a surface-to-air missile and a flamethrower, but also petty issues like the thirty-round AR15 magazines, in the end he decided not to pursue the issue since the public sentiment was overwhelmingly on our side. And that would be bad for politics.

Cora and I had not only defended our town against some very evil people, we'd fallen in love in the process. It was a love story for the ages. As my new Manhattan-based literary agent put it, ours was "a story that had all the drama, conflict, action, and romance of a Hemingway novel." Cora and I had survived a modern-day For Whom the Bell Tolls, and because of it, the book and movie offers were rolling it. In a word, Cora and I were getting rich, but we didn't act like it.

Sheriff Woods never did get the chance to give me the one-hundred K he owed me, but then, I not only didn't need it anymore, he died trying to save Cora's and my life, and I would be forever grateful to his memory.

Ironically, the little sleepy town of Loon Lake became a major tourist attraction. Investors were pouring in. The place had been quickly cleaned up, the buildings leveled while new, far bigger and more modern building complexes were being constructed. Even the old insurance building that we'd utilized as The Alamo was turned into a museum dedicated to the Battle of Loon Lake. There were three floors of exhibits, a fifteen-minute filmed documentary, and the damaged wall that had been hit by the state trooper rocket was left intact. It was the museum's most dramatic display.

Loon Lake was now being considered as a possible site for the 2040 Winter Olympic Games, not that I'd live long enough to see it. Bunny's Place was booming, and the walls of her reconstructed business were covered with newspaper and magazine accounts of the battle. The AR15 she'd used in the battle was now mounted proudly over the bar back. Cora and I received more offers for Loon Lake Inn than we could count. Some of them so lucrative they made our mouths water, but in the end, we didn't sell out. Truth is, we refused to sell out.

Now that the town was turning into a big attraction

with new hotels, restaurants, a multiplex movie theater, and even a Play-O-Rama complex with go-carts, batting cages, and waterslide facility, we wanted to keep the inn in its original rustic form. Naturally, we were booked up for going on three years, and we could pretty much charge what we wanted for the nightly rentals of the cabins. But it was our home now, and nothing could change that. Not even money and fame.

Cora and I even kept the cabin beyond the pines situated away from the others as our own. We still enjoyed sleeping there, drinking red wine in bed, making love until we were exhausted, and in the morning, getting up early and drinking coffee down on the small dock while the fish jumped in the lake and the birds sang and circled around us. Because we'd rid ourselves of Sonny Torchi and defended Loon Lake, our lives had become nothing short of idyllic.

When the blue and yellow prowler showed up in the inn's parking lot, I had no doubt who was seated behind the wheel, nor was I surprised to see him. Because it was inevitable that he would show back up one day. He got out of the car, looking big and serious, especially when he put his gray Stetson on, pulling the brim far enough down on his forehead that it somewhat concealed his intense eyes. I walked out onto the tavern porch while he slowly approached the steps.

"Good afternoon, Lieutenant Spencer," I said. "I've been expecting you."

"Mind if I come in?" he asked politely.

"I've got fresh coffee going," I said. Then, smiling wryly, "Unless, that is, you prefer something stronger."

"Coffee is fine," he said, climbing the three steps and following me inside.

I got the coffee and set it out for him on the bar while I stood facing him from the bar back. He sipped the coffee and pursed his lips.

"It's good," he said. "What kind is it?"

"Death Wish Coffee," I said. "It's supposed to have the most caffeine of any coffee out there. Won a bunch of awards.

Only the best for you, Lieutenant."

He stared into his cup contemplatively.

"That's not a metaphor, is it, Mr. Kingsley?" he asked. "Death wish, I mean."

"Not at all." I smiled. "It's just good coffee. That's all."

He cleared the frog in his throat. "You and Cora have become genuine celebrities," he said. "You're rich, you're famous, you're healthy, despite that blood bath of a battle. I guess you could say you two are the best thing not only to happen to one another but to Loon Lake in general."

"I like to think so, Lieutenant," I said. "These days, I live the simple life of the caretaker."

He sipped his coffee.

"That's funny," he said.

"What's funny?" I said.

"I'm told that's what Sonny Torchi always referred to himself as."

"The caretaker."

"Precisely," he said. "And now you have the caretaker's wife, don't you?"

I smiled. "Guess you could say that. But I'm just a writer who also runs an inn."

He sipped more coffee, wiped his mouth with the back of his hand.

"He was left-handed, you know."

"I'm sorry?" I said.

"Sonny Torchi. You know, Loon Lake Inn's original caretaker. He was left-handed. Which is why the massive cut he suffered on his left thigh was inconsistent with a left-handed man. Strange, isn't it?"

That's when I felt the goosebumps rise on my skin. It was almost like a frigid wind had just blown in through the door.

"Something else was strange, too," he went on. "The way the flesh was cut. It was slashed at an upward angle, which, of course, would be impossible for a man to accomplish by himself. That is, unless he was a professional contortionist." He snickered. "A chainsaw blade revolves around its housing in a clockwise fashion, but the gash on Sonny's thigh indicates that it was made when the blade was going counter-clockwise. You see, Kingsley, when he was cut, the machine was being held upside down. No way big Sonny Torchi was a contortionist. Not with that big belly."

In my head, I relived the moment I cut Sonny. I saw myself burying the screaming blade in his thigh. It never dawned on me one way or the other that the forensics experts could figure out which direction the blade was spinning when it cut into his thigh. But I could have kicked myself for not anticipating it.

"Well, I'll be damned," I whispered to myself.

The front door opened slowly. So slowly, it was like it wasn't being opened at all. More like I imagined it being opened up. Cora slipped inside, began tiptoeing toward the bar. In her hand, she held a French knife. The blade glistened in the ray of sunlight that shined in through the door opening.

The dying Sonny Torchi came immediately to mind. *"Well, you'll soon...find out...what Cora's all about. She's... no better...than me."*

"So, if I were to come to a logical conclusion," the lieutenant went on, "I would say you knew that if Sonny cut himself badly enough in the thigh, he'd sever his femoral artery and bleed out on the spot. At least, that's what you were going for when you purposely cut him with the chainsaw."

I turned then, pulled the bottle of Irish whiskey off the bar back. I got a clean glass from under the bar and poured myself a shot.

"How about a sweetener for your Death Wish Coffee, Lieutenant Spencer?" I said. "It's got to be five o'clock somewhere."

He grinned, shook his head.

"I never drink on duty," he said. "I'm one of the good cops. Not like those cops who were on Sonny's payroll. Sonny is better off dead, that's the truth. And between you and me, Mr. Kingsley, I don't mind saying that you did the world a great big favor when you murdered him in his own cold blood. And that's why I'm here, on my own, to let you be the first to know that I know exactly what you did to Sonny Torchi out there on Loon Lake Trail. Not even the county DA knows, not the press, not nobody. Just you and me. And you can take that shit to the bank."

I downed my shot and poured another. Cora was only a few feet away from the state trooper now. Her eyes were glaring into mine, unblinking, determined, unforgiving. I knew what she was about to do, and I knew that in her heart, there was no way she was going to allow this one policeman the chance to upset our lives. Our perfect, idyllic lives. Not after everything we fought for. Not a chance in hell.

"But the law is the law, Mr. Kingsley," the lieutenant went on unapologetically. "And I can't keep our secret a secret for very long. The law must be respected, or I would be no better than those men and women who betrayed the state trooper oath. That said, I must insist that you allow me to take you in without a struggle." He shook his head, almost sadly, bit down on his bottom lip. "To be perfectly honest, I nearly let this one slide. I almost let it go because Sonny was such a bad man. But in the end, I spoke to God, and God spoke back to me. And you know what he said, Mr. Kingsley?"

For a long beat, I looked into Spencer's big brown eyes. "I bet God said, 'Lieutenant Spencer, you most definitely have a death wish.'"

His eyes grew extra wide as the long razor-sharp blade cut his neck wide open like an overly ripe melon. The blood spurted out and he grabbed hold of his throat, and his eyes never blinked nor did they stop focusing on mine while he choked and drowned in his own dark red blood.

Of course, he wasn't able to talk. I didn't have much to say to him anyway, other than goodbye. But here's the million dollar question: was the Trooper lying when he said he was one of the good guys in all of this? Because maybe I should have felt bad about what we did to him. Correction, what we had no choice in doing.

But in the end, I felt at peace. I trusted his every word when he said he never told anyone about Sonny's murder. But at the same time, I knew he was also lying through his teeth about being one of the good troopers. And now, I was about to prove it.

"Cora," I said. "Do you have Sonny's phone?"

"I have a bag of his stuff the funeral parlor gave me after they cremated what was left of his body."

"Grab it and the charger," I said.

Smartly, she made her way to the front door and locked it. Then she entered her office. She came back with a smartphone in hand along with a black charger. She went around the bar and plugged the charger into an outlet located on the bar back. She plugged the charger into the phone and brought it to life. She entered a four-digit code into the phone's security portal.

"You know Sonny's PIN?" I asked.

"It's his birthday," she explained. "What is it you need to see? Whatever it is, be quick. We have a dead body bleeding all over the place."

"I think you know what I want to see," I said.

"I don't know if I can look at it," she said.

I took the phone from her and went to pictures and videos. When I found what I wanted, I tapped the icon with my fingertip, and the video came to life. My blood was pounding because what I saw not only broke my heart, but it confirmed every suspicion I had in my bones about Lt. Spencer. The video was shaky because Sonny was holding the smartphone in his hand and moving around a lot. But it showed the Kennedy family duct taped to the chairs in their kitchen. The kitchen was on fire, and so were the Kennedys. They were screaming in agony.

But at one point, Sonny turned the camera on himself. He was laughing so hard he was crying. Big Billy was standing behind him. He was also laughing. Four more men entered into the frame. They were state troopers. One of them was a black man. It was Lt. Spencer. He wasn't laughing. None of the troopers were laughing. But then, they weren't doing anything to stop the family from burning up either. They weren't attempting to arrest Sonny or Big Billy. They were just standing there watching the gruesome scene.

Until Lt. Spencer called out to Sonny.

"We've got to get the hell out of here before the fire flashes," he shouted.

"So much for fun," Sonny said. Then, speaking directly into the camera, "This is what happens when you defy Sonny Torchi. You get torched. Get it?"

Just before the video ended, you could hear Sonny's squeaky laughter as it drowned out the screams and cries of the dying.

"What my husband did to that family was murder," Cora said. "They were all murderers. Sonny and Big Billy got what they had coming. Lt. Spencer got what he had coming."

"And Sheriff Woods?" I said. "Did he know all along that Spencer was one of the troopers complicit in the Kennedy family murders?"

"What the hell could he do about it, Kingsley?" she said. "What the hell could I do?"

"I guess you just had to wait around until someone like me came along. A drifter with a stainless steel spine and not a thing in the world to lose."

"We needed someone who would kill Sonny," she said. "Someone we could trust without question. Someone who would help us fight Sonny's family. Somebody who would fight for us."

"But it's still murder," I said, watching the trooper bleed out on the floor. "But I guess, sometimes murder is the right thing to do."

But murder was also a messy business if nothing else. I used to write crime novels that romanticized murder. Trust me when I say there's not a single romantic thing about it. We had to clean the place up and keep the tourists a safe enough distance away, which meant closing the tavern for the day under the excuse of a leaky gas line. The bar, the barstool the trooper occupied, and the floor had to be scrubbed and disinfected. I even thought about replacing some of the floorboards, but my gut told me that Lieutenant Spencer was not fibbing when he said he came here of his own accord, meaning he never told a soul where he was heading when he left the state trooper barracks off Exit 28 to make his way to Loon Lake Inn. Correction, maybe God knew and perhaps the devil, but that's as far as the chain extended.

We dragged the body down to the onion cellar. Pulling the trooper's wallet from his pants pocket and his smartphone from his shirt pocket, I shoved them inside my own pockets.

We then made our way back upstairs. When we were sure none of the vacationers were watching, we got in the state trooper cruiser and drove it out of the parking lot and to the main road. Without giving it a second thought, our plan was to dump the car in Lake Champlain, which was only a few miles up the road. We knew this would be the trickiest part of the operation since the vehicle might be electronically tracked with GPS and we might pass by another trooper cruiser. Which was why I decided to don the Lieutenant's Stetson— which was two sizes too big so that I had to keep pushing it up on my forehead—while I drove. At the same time, I made Cora scrunch down in her seat so that she wouldn't be spotted should the worst happen.

When we came to a spot in the road that not only offered a great view of the massive lake but that also abutted a sheer vertical cliffside drop into the lake of one-hundred feet or more, I hit the brakes. Turning onto the soft shoulder, I plowed through the wood safety barrier. Then I threw the vehicle in park and kept the engine running.

"Hurry," I said to Cora.

"Do you think this will really work?" she asked.

"The vehicle is made mostly of iron. She'll sink, believe me."

When I gave her the word, I shifted the prowler into neutral and together, Cora and I pushed the vehicle over the side. For a brief second, we stared into one another's eyes while we waited for the tell-tale splash. It was a big splash, let me tell you, and it caused us both to smile. We made our way to the edge of the cliff and we watched the cruiser slowly fill with lake water until it disappeared under the lake's surface just like the Titanic did in the North Atlantic all those years ago.

Walking back to the road, Cora said, "Won't the state troopers get suspicious when they find out one of their cars is missing and the lieutenant along with it? I mean, the barrier is busted. They'll put two and two together and figure out the cruiser might be at the bottom of the lake."

We walked along the road back in the direction of Loon Lake. Cora was an ex-cop, and presently she was thinking like one.

"They'll eventually figure it out," I said. "But when they do, it will have nothing to do with you and me. They'll just figure Lieutenant Spencer was either murdered by some gang member and his car ditched in the lake, or maybe they'll even figure he killed himself over something he did wrong… something so bad he could no longer live with himself. He drove into the lake, and the fish got to his body. Let me tell you something, Cora, there's fish in Lake Champlain that are so big they would scare the daylights out of you."

"Okay, Kingsley," Cora said, taking hold my hand. "If I were still a cop investigating the missing lieutenant, I might get suspicious. But what choice did we have but to handle things the way we did?"

"Are you worried?" I asked.

"If you're not worried, I'm not worried," she said.

The Caretaker's Wife

We walked the full four and a half miles back to Loon Lake with our happy faces on, like we'd been out for one of our long, midday hikes in the great outdoors.

The really messy stuff took place later that day down in the onion cellar where we cut the trooper's body up into manageable parts and then bagged them in Hefty garbage bags. I made a fire in a fifty-gallon drum out back of the tavern, far enough away from the cottages. While the happy vacationing families enjoyed the beach, the fishing, the sail boating, and the hiking on the Loon Lake Trail, we burned up every bit of the body, until all that was left was ash and little fragments of bone and teeth.

Here's what I also did. I retrieved Lt. Spencer's wallet from my jeans pocket. I slid out one of his business cards. Then, attaching a copy of the Kennedy family murder video to his state trooper email, I pressed send. I repeated the process with his cell phone address, forwarding the video as a multi-media text. When I was finished, I tossed both his wallet and his smartphone into the still roaring fire. I held on to his semi-automatic and his utility belt, which I would dump in Loon Lake at a later date. Eventually, there would be an investigation into the disappearance of Lt. Spencer, and they would discover the video and the trooper's complicity in the horrible quadruple homicide. My guess was that when the trooper cruiser was finally discovered lying at the bottom of Lake Champlain, it would be deduced that Spencer had, in fact, killed himself over grief about his role in the murders. It wasn't a fool-proof conclusion, but it wasn't totally off the rails either.

Later on, after getting much of the evening's dinner offerings going, including a hearty homemade creamy mushroom soup and a venison stew (Sonny's old recipe), I dug a deep hole and buried the ashy remnants of Lieutenant Spencer's body. As I filled in the hole, I thought about saying a few prayers, but then decided against it. I wasn't so sure the good Lord above would want to hear from me after the violent manner in which we took the Trooper's life, but if there was something I wanted to say to God directly, it was this. Yes, Cora and I killed the lieutenant, but it wasn't personal. It was just business. A God-awful messy business. And what the hell, he had it coming.

After the hole was filled in, I spread corn seeds all around a flat area of land that was maybe twenty by thirty. It was a piece of ground that got plenty of sunlight, and that wasn't disturbed by the old thick roots from the many pine, oak, and birch trees surrounding the property. I knew I could grow myself a really nice crop of corn there. Not only had I read about a murderer who planted a crop of corn over a woman he'd murdered and then buried in the garden, but I also knew that if customers of Loon Lake tavern loved one thing with their home cooked dinners, it was fresh ears of corn.

Did I fail to mention that Cora is pregnant? She's going to have our baby in a few months. We're so excited about the news. We don't know if it's going to be a girl or a boy, and being the old-fashioned type, we don't want to know. We want it to be a total surprise. We've begun construction on a good-sized addition to the private cabin beyond the trees. We're adding a nursery to it, and another full bath, plus a wrap-around porch for sitting outside. But it's still going to be our cozy home away from it all. A place filled with peace and love. It will be everything I ever wanted. A loyal wife who needs me and a child who loves me.

Life…it can be a wonderful thing. I've won some, and I've allowed some very precious things to slip through my fingers like fine sand. God knows I've been lucky. You might even say I've been blessed.

Yes, I just might be the luckiest man alive.

About the Author

Winner of the 2015 PWA Shamus Award and the 2015 ITW Thriller Award for Best Original Paperback Novel for *Moonlight Weeps*, Vincent Zandri is the *New York Times*, *USA Today*, and Amazon Kindle Overall No.1 bestselling author of more than 40 novels and novellas, including *The Remains*, *Everything Burns*, *Orchard Grove* and the *The Detonator*.

Zandri's list of domestic publishers include Delacorte, Dell, Down & Out Books, Thomas & Mercer, and Polis Books. An MFA in writing graduate of Vermont College, Zandri's work has been translated into Dutch, Russian, French, Italian, Japanese, and Polish. Recently, Zandri was the subject of a major feature by the *New York Times*.

He has also made appearances on Bloomberg TV and the Fox News Network. In December 2014, *Suspense Magazine* named Zandri's *The Shroud Key* as one of the Best Books of 2014. Recently, *Suspense Magazine* selected *When Shadows Come* as one of the Best Books of 2016.

A freelance photojournalist and the author of the popular lit blog, The Vincent Zandri Vox, Zandri has written for *Living Ready Magazine, RT, New York Newsday, Hudson Valley Magazine, Writers Digest, The Times Union* (Albany), *Game & Fish Magazine*, and many more.

He lives in Albany, New York and Florence, Italy. For more, go to www.VincentZandri.com.